COMMON
CARNAGE

BOOKS BY STEPHEN DOBYNS

Stephen Dobyns

PENGUIN POETS

COMMON
CARNAGE

PENGUIN BOOKS
Published by the Penguin Group
Penguin Books USA Inc., 375 Hudson Street, New York,
New York 10014, U.S.A.
Penguin Books Ltd, 27 Wrights Lane, London W8 5TZ, England
Penguin Books Australia Ltd, Ringwood, Victoria, Australia
Penguin Books Canada Ltd, 10 Alcorn Avenue,
Toronto, Ontario, Canada M4V 3B2
Penguin Books (N.Z.) Ltd, 182–190 Wairau Road,
Auckland 10, New Zealand

Penguin Books Ltd, Registered Offices: Harmondsworth,
Middlesex, England

First published in Penguin Books 1996

10 9 8 7 6 5 4 3 2 1

Copyright © Stephen Dobyns, 1996
All rights reserved

Pages ix–x constitute an extension of this copyright page.

Library of Congress Cataloging-in-Publication Data
Dobyns, Stephen, 1941–
Common carnage / Stephen Dobyns.
p.   cm.
ISBN 0 14 05.8748 9 (pbk.)
I. Title.
PS3554.02C59   1996
811'.54—dc20   95-30214

Printed in the United States of America
Set in Bembo
Designed by Katy Riegel

For my mother:
Barbara Dobyns

Preguntaréis: Y dónde están las lilas?
Y la metafísica cubierta de amapolas?
Y la lluvia que a menudo golpeaba
sus palabras llenándolas
de agujeros y pájaros?

PABLO NERUDA
"EXPLICO ALGUNAS COSAS"

I have been born of the same as the war was born.

WALT WHITMAN
"TO A CERTAIN CIVILIAN"

ACKNOWLEDGMENTS

Acknowledgments are due to the editors of the following publications, in whose pages many of the poems in this book first appeared.

Agni Review: "Best in the Business"

Alaska Quarterly Review: "Ancient Teaching," "Homeric Offering," "Sketching Hector's Eye," "What They Do Always"

Antaeus: "Painful Fingers"

The American Poetry Review: "Allegorical Matters," "Art et Al.," "Crimson Invitation," "Digging the Knife Deeper," "Golden Broilers," "Gutter Trouble," "Hopeless Tools," "Indifference to Consequence," "Nouns of Assemblage," "Pushing Ahead," "Who Is Mistaken?" "Winter Nights"

Black Warrior Review: "Education," "Heaven"

Borderlands: "Let's Take a Break"

Boulevard: "Nocturnal Obstruction"

Colorado Review: "Street Smart"

Cream City Review: "Bad Luck Fence"

DoubleTake: "Thelonious Monk"

Exquisite Corpse: "Lullaby"

The Georgia Review: "The Privileges of Philosophy," "Quiet Time"

The Gettysburg Review: "Lil' Darlin'," "Middle-Aged Black Men"

Green Mountain Review: "The Big Difference," "Pink Spot," "Street Racket"

Greensboro Review: "Artistic Matters," "Dead Poet Ha Ha"

The Harvard Review: "Second Skin"

Hiram Review: "Fade Out," "The Monster," "What's That, Who's There?" "Widened Horizons"

The Hudson Review: "Rattletrap," "When a Friend"

The Iowa Review: "Trying Not to Be Cynical"

The Marlboro Review: "Odysseus Discusses Achilles," "Sex Before Dog," "Uninvited"

New England Review: "Being Happy," "Getting Tougher"

North American Review: "Cold Marble," "Primavera"

Northeast Corridor: "Dead Dreaming," "The World as Textbook"

The Paris Review: "Garden Bouquet," "Then What Is the Question?"

Phoebe: "Santiago: Plaza de Armas"

Poems & Plays: "Back to School," "Casualties of April," "The Invitations Overhead," "The Rotations of the Earth"

Salmagundi: "Bead Curtain," "His Decision," "No Hands"

Salt Hill Journal: "The Impossible"

San Diego Reader: "Hans Ironfoot et Al."

Virginia Quarterly Review: "Consolations of Water," "To Keep One's Treasure Protected," "Visitor"

CONTENTS

COMMON
CARNAGE

WINTER NIGHTS

Like day laborers bunched around a construction site
as dawn breaks, the souls of the unborn cluster
high above the stratosphere waiting to be chosen.
From earth they appear as points of light: their
radiant glitter indicating an eagerness to be born.
Each day many are rejected and briefly their light
dims, yet repeatedly they brighten as hope returns.

One night from a restaurant window, I watched two boys,
perhaps five and eight, wash all the windshields
of the cars parked along the street. Then they settled
on the curb to wait. They had no doubt that soon
a car owner would come and they would politely
request a little coin. They were young; it was late.
Their hope was a red blossom they knew would open.

I think of my friends who died young. The suicide
of a woman who loved to laugh. Death by cancer
of a man in the midst of great work. Other friends
whose ambitions came to naught. The divorces,
the fierce blows between former lovers, the timid
retreat into drunkenness, eccentricity and complaint.
Look, our memories are stuffed with such stories!

At times on winter nights the souls of the unborn
appear as fireworks. No moon, the snow stretching
its cold unbroken carpet to the black line of trees.
Above, the swirling pinwheels of multicolored lights
burn as eagerly as fanned sparks bursting into fire.
How could I live without their example, the sweet
and ever so fragile expectation of happiness?

THE PRIVILEGES OF PHILOSOPHY

Two barn owls discuss Descartes as they
disembowel a field mouse without the help
of knife or fork. They are friends and
share even the tastiest bits. For instance,
each gets one lung. Sum, says one. Ergo
cogito, says the other. Then they chuckle.
The night is cold; the fields are white.

The owls perch on the branch of an old oak
and survey the moonlit landscape where voles
and field mice, where even the rabbits pass
on tiptoe and shush one another. Sum fierce
ergo sum, says one barn owl. Sum terrible
ergo sum, says the other. Their laughter
drifts across the snow-covered fields. If we

stepped back and painted this scene or just took
a snapshot—the moon above the dilapidated
barn, the angular bare branches of maples
and oaks, the rolling white fields with snow
halfway up the fence posts—this could serve
as a fitting picture for a calendar, the sort
to make even the most cynical pilgrim pause

in his long march and sigh. Yet here as well
there is unpleasantness. The Big Folks chuckle
and pat their backs, the Little scuttle from
snowdrift to snowdrift. Between courses,
the Big amuse themselves with highbrow talk,
but the Little have no time for books. Their
bellies are always half empty, they are always

in a hurry, even asleep they see the owl's
dark shadow dropping upon them. Sum monster ergo
cogito, says one owl to his pal, their laughter
floats on the still winter air, happy killers
who love their chat and love their children.
On the barn wall, the thermometer jerks awake,
shivers, yawns, then drops another two degrees.

THEN WHAT IS THE QUESTION?

It is hard to think of the people of Thebes
as being fortunate (so much time has gone by),
but they possessed a machine of exact measure:
a monster with the head and breasts of a woman,
body of a lion, wings of a bird, serpent's tail,
a lion's paws and a sweet human voice: the Sphinx,
a sort of savage bureaucrat who kept life on track,

asking questions of the passersby. Those unable
to gather the answer became lunch. Functional
Darwinism. Who knows what strains of stupidity
were deleted from the Theban gene pool when some
cheerful dummy rubbed his jaw and said, Beats me.
Only Oedipus got the answer right. "What goes
on four feet, on two feet, on three. But the more

feet it goes on the weaker it be." The point is
the Sphinx was a fixed spot on the road. Tourists
could take her picture had there been cameras.
Sad to say, these days the Sphinx is invisible,
but even hungrier. Young and pretty, old and ugly—
the Sphinx devours them all. Victims of Violence,
reads the newspaper, Unknown Assailants,

Mysterious Motives. The cops scratch their heads.
Not only is the Sphinx hidden from us, but also
we don't know the riddle—a new one this time.
You ask why poets stand at the crossroads shouting
single words: Hypotenuse, Zebra, Waffle Iron!
These are possible answers to a question which
remains secret or has yet to be asked. A foolish

endeavor, you suggest. But imagine the feather
in the cap of the poet who gets it right. Snow
Flake, Radish, Toe-box! Abruptly the killing stops:
a feeling of buoyancy, the sense that it is okay
to go outdoors. No more drive-by shootings or murder
in the night. History books argue that the death
of the Theban Sphinx led to the flowering of the arts

in ancient Greece. Be that as it may, all we know
for sure is that our Sphinx is like a pane of glass
between us and the sun, or perhaps a gossamer web
in the clouds above us, or a single vicious drop
of water in an otherwise kindly sea. Perhaps someday
she will tire of life incognito and reveal herself.
Perhaps she will articulate the riddle and we can

put the computers to work. Poets will stop shouting
Rutabaga, Doorstop! We can join together in a kindly
manner to discover the answer. Those Thebans: how we
should envy them! Their Sphinx was three-dimensional.
Her claws sparkled in the sunlight. Her laughter woke
babies in their cribs. For good or ill, you always
knew what questions to answer, what roads to avoid.

HEADLONG RUSH

Sometimes we can stare so hard
that the object of our gaze—
a woman's face, birch trees

near a waterfall, a painting
of apples around a blue vase—
will seem no longer fleeting.

What does it mean, the word Eternal?
Staring at some scene, we can think,
briefly, that it has always rested

before us. Looking into the shadows
of a woman's eyes can spark a moment
with neither beginning nor end.

Or a painting may so ignite us
that the minute will be blown open
and we wander dazed across the blue

checked cloth and curves of red fruit.
How dangerous are such occasions.
They impede our headlong rush

by keeping us from imagining
those bright targets against which
we hope to cast our shot.

Don't our goals always lie ahead?
Aren't we enemies of the stationary?
But in this glance we sometimes

find all we have lost, all we
have forced ourselves to set aside:
the pool at the bottom of the falls,

the froth of white water and the wind
tossing the white branches of the birch.
How can we do ourselves such injury?

How can we possibly turn away?
Yet we do. Our motion defines us.
We are the creatures who rush forward

on narrow roads toward darkness.
What do we lose? It is our own lives
that fall away on the roads behind us.

THE ROTATIONS OF THE EARTH

She loves him, he loves someone else,
male or female, who's to say? And that
other casts an eye on still another.
Thus they proceed across the planet,

as a string of elephants ambles
through a jungle: trunk to tail. Just
how many live like this, propelled
by yearning's little motor? You'd

think their eyes would be fixed
on the sidewalk before them. Not true.
They watch the horizon. Let's say
their desires got remixed and all

located the single lover they wanted.
Wouldn't the world come to a halt, plunged
into one long hiatus of pleasure? But
that's not our nature; rather, we exist

like a man in a crowd given a push
and staggering off kilter, trying to
recover his footing. People stand back.
Is he in danger? This isn't progress

exactly, nor is he napping. The eggheads
call it flux, others call it dancing,
a point between the ecstatic and erratic.
Poets call it mimesis. For how else did we

learn the art of constant variation, if not
from the planet itself: life through gyration.
For doesn't sex make us spin from flirtation
to fornication, to new infatuation again?

GETTING TOUGHER

In the workshop for transitional children
menacing faces are fashioned from wax,
then bones are formed from fabric and sticks,
muscular arms and a torso hanging down.

The faces are painted, made grim, given a hat—
look, these aren't guys you'd want to fight.
At last a harness is attached to the back
and the puppet (what else to call it?) is all set.

Let's follow one out to the street. The child
hoists the frame onto his shoulders and staggers
into a crowd jam-packed with similar creatures.
How terrible are their faces. The children yell,

shake the puppets at each other. They swagger.
Frequently the child returns to the factory
to have his puppet's ugly kisser made uglier,
add a surly glare, a scar. Truly it's a monster,

but under the machinery, lipstick and paint
the child is hunkered down, trying to figure
what to do next, how to live, how to endure
the loneliness. Years pass. Solitude accumulates.

As the puppet gets meaner, it gets heavier.
The child wants to let it drop but then who
would protect him? The child hasn't a clue.
By now the puppet has a creased brow, cruel stare,

a lopsided smirk lit by a wreckage of dental work.
Doesn't this show the child has won his battle?
From the outside we imagine a soul utterly brutal,
but on the inside the child only feels burnt out.

Then his costume is taken from him, placed in
a hole in the ground and the child at last resigns.
How light he feels as he hurries onto green lawns
where the sun is rising and his friends waiting.

PAINFUL FINGERS

In the Museum of the Ethical Neutrality of Tools,
Billy the Kid's six-gun rests on a red cushion
like a virgin anticipating the caresses
of her first lover. The razor of Jack the Ripper

wonders what the fuss is about. The dagger
of Lady Macbeth drowsily dreams of fog-smeared
hills and the Hey-what-the-heck attitude of sheep.
Racks of bombs, boxes of grenades, glass cases

of tommy guns, brass knuckles, executioners' axes
variously contemplate trips to the beach, nights
staring up at the stars, the innocent delight
of hearing an old lady's giddy and abandoned laugh.

And there in the corner, in a place of honor,
the sword of Achilles neither broods nor weeps.
Taffeta tints drift through its childish sensibilities.
For us the past was murder; it felt it was dancing.

Don't go near it! Do you see the guard at the exit
with the bandaged hand? Mistakenly, believing
himself secure, he unlocked the padlocked door.
Who could have told him the blade still burned?

for Joel Brouwer

THE WORLD AS TEXTBOOK

The snake strikes the boot. The scorpion
rams its sting repeatedly into the thorax
of a wasp. A knot of ants drags off a fly.
The mind modifies the world to metaphor,
then relates all events back to itself.

All day the cat hunts birds among the roses.
And what hunts me? What do I hunt? The souls
of the vicious, souls of the kind—don't
they linger around us just to caution us?
To forget the world is to become its victim.

See how the barbed wire slices and grabs—
can't I take a lesson from this? The souls
of the jealous, souls of the loving—how
sharp is a mouthful of vinegar, how sweet
is a few drops. The peonies give their beauty

to the garden as the ants suck their juice—
think of the wisdom to be found there. Do I
live by letting the clock push me forward?
Are one's fellow creatures only merchandise?
Do I let myself be used up, then cast away?

The souls of the greedy, souls of the mild:
these hermit crabs on the beach, how they hide
in borrowed houses. The gulls swoop down and
snatch them, drop them on rocks and smash them.
I am surrounded by unpleasant information

against which I set a mountain of distraction:
sex and money, the society's sweet diversions.
The TV flicks off—Wake up, it's time to die!
Where am I running to, where have I been?
My breath is used up even as I sleep.

DEAD DREAMING

In the luggage room of the secondhand shop
battered suitcases are stacked to the ceiling,
canvas and pigskin, vinyl, cardboard and plastic.

These are the fat souls, those who loved deeply.
See how their sides are bloated with feeling.
Fat souls—consider their intense dreaming.

See how their corners are scuffed up, locks broken.
Fat souls—still stuffed with the recollection
of sweet destinations. Consider the plans that led

to their purchase: vacations, hoped-for moments,
the lovers' weekends at the sea. Hair ribbons
and grains of sand still hide in side pockets.

In some there lingers the whiff of perfume.
Long dead is the woman who wore this scent.
Touch the folds of the pink satin lining.

Consider their glances and eager unpacking.
Consider her lover as he undressed her.
Suitcases bursting with lush expectation—

each one richest during days of transition.
Fat souls packed up to start a new life.
Dragged through airports and train stations—

each is the enactment of something expected,
each embraces the uncertain and unprotected:
tomorrow's cornucopia, tomorrow's defeat.

Seams stretched to encompass a dead reverie,
escaping the known for the mystery. Fat souls—
into the dark with their hearts neatly folded.

ART ET AL.

Four men shoot craps in an alley, crouched
on the concrete. Suddenly they hear a shout
and a fifth man comes dashing toward them,
leaps across the dice tossers and smacks

into the brick wall head-first. The sound
of his dome banging the brick makes a smack
like a loaf of bread might make if dropped
from a rooftop to a sidewalk. The gamblers

gather the coins strewn by the man's feet
and glance to see if he's dead. He sprawls
without moving a nostril. The others return
to their game. Box cars, says one. Money

is exchanged. The man on the ground moans
and stands up. The gamblers roll their eyes
in vexation. The man totters down the alley,
pressing his palms to his brain. These aren't

young guys and their clothing isn't the best.
All need haircuts and shaves, need their shoes
resoled. Then they hear another shout and once
more the fifth man comes galloping toward them.

The dice are grabbed up just as the man dives
across their game and strikes the wall, whack,
cranium-first. The noise his head makes is like
the noise a boot makes, crunching a walnut.

Someone rolls the dice. Lady luck be with me now,
says a gambler. The man on his back groans,
gets to his feet and staggers down the alley.
The dice players raise their eyebrows and make

"what-next?" expressions. From this we may guess
the craps and behavior of the peculiar kibitzer
have gone on all morning. And in the next hour,
it happens five more times. They hear the shout,

the slap-slap of shoes getting louder, they see
the man's determined expression as he dives
across their game, then, splat, the sound
of a head striking the brick. Briefly, the others

feel hope. Has he busted his neck? Then,
with a moan, the man gets up and does it again.
It's hard to say who suffers most. None
of these guys lead happy lives and one way

or another each has made an adjustment to despair
and surrender, evil thoughts and failure. Some
shoot craps, others bust their noggin and the line
dividing them is more philosophical than physical.

Then one joker drags a Dumpster over to the wall.
This time when the fifth man comes barreling
down the alley, his head, on impact, creates
a pleasing bong. Of course no work of art achieves

perfection without modification and the Dumpster
has to be fine tuned, moved to the left, emptied
of half its contents but soon when the man
comes running, his forehead striking the metal

makes a pristine chiming noise which resonates
through the courtyard and sends a chill of pleasure
down the backs of the four men. The clang of his brain
banging the hollow Dumpster is like a chord swiped

from a Bartók concerto: agreeable to the ears,
uplifting for the soul. Now when the man sprawls
on the concrete the others wish him well. They
help him to his feet and make little salutes

as he staggers away. Even here, in an alley
at the end of the world, art has its celebrants,
those who suffer to make it, those who make
the suffering their own, because for each man

the unique whack recalls a painful moment,
as if it hung before them, sparkling in the air.
One man thinks of a mother, long dead. One thinks
of a first wife, long unseen. Children, sunsets,

uncompromised youth, promises kept. Later when
the cop on the beat wanders into the alley
he discovers the dice players dreaming happily.
Drugs? he thinks, Too much cheap wine? Suddenly,

the fifth man comes sprinting toward them,
the footsteps get louder, there's a brief silence
as the man goes airborne, then, Boing, his skull
slams the metal and the sound drifts up to wake

the rats from their slumber, disturb the pigeons
at their endless breakfast. The four men make
little sighs of pleasure. Any cop will tell you
he has seen it all, but for pure sadistic delight

this takes the cake and the cop slaps the guys
in irons. In the paddy wagon, their leader keeps
shouting about Art, but the cop knows all about Art.
He's seen his mug shot on a thousand post office walls:

a dangerous perpetrator of disreputable behavior
who stays one jump ahead of the law. But this time
the cop is confident. Now that he has caught his gang
can Art hide out much longer? The cop thinks not.

SEX BEFORE DOG

If ignorance is a wall around us,
then where is the door through which
truth enters? And do such doors exist?

Perhaps one is in those few moments
after orgasm as the world trickles
back and before irony has the chance

to reassert itself, before self-
deception once more puts its delicate
pinkie over the controls. How green

and virginal is the world at that time.
Again possibility points out the path
through the maze that so befuddles us

during those hours we walk up-straight.
And where does truth enter this scenario
as we lie naked and alert? Isn't truth

the light kindling the landscape at dawn?
Not that it reveals the answers, but
it creates the illusion that we might

decipher what gets told. And the message?
Only to linger loyally, like a mutt tied
to a parking meter waiting for its ten-

year-old owner to exit the movie theater,
this hot Saturday afternoon in July. But
to the mutt it's just a doorway and time

is that span between the emptying and
filling of a food dish, because it's not
truth but the arrival of a phantasm

resembling truth in those velvety moments
after sex: the faith to keep believing,
the pluck to stay patient, the hope of being

taken for a long walk. And won't it happen?
Won't the movie end and the kid exit? But these
are jiffies only, bat whispers sent to make us

feel buoyant before the world rams itself back
into our life and we collapse to the sidewalk,
to yawn, to philosophize, to harass our fleas.

DEAD POET HA HA

The bird on the branch was singing of gladness,
disrupting my dreams with its dreadful screech.
Rushing outside I knocked it from its perch
with one blow of the garden rake. What madness!
shouted my neighbors. Quickly they filled the yard.
Long had I been the object of their scrutiny.
Long had they waited for this opportunity.
At my trial they alleged I had spread discord
in the neighborhood; I had even flung mud
at their block party with my poetry: a litany
of rhymed dirty jokes leading to their mutiny.
The judge shook his head. Hadn't I understood
the last lyric poet had hanged himself in 1914?
He showed his snapshot: a gloomy fellow, slack
jawed, cracked glasses, gray cheeks across which
some clown had drawn eggy tears in blue crayon.
But I had already seen the video adaptation,
where the poet toasted with a sonnet the odorous
conflagration of his neighbor's outhouse
which he mistook for the sunset: his confusion
enacts the perversion of art, that the faux pas
sparking the poet's farewell inflames my inspiration!

WIDENED HORIZONS

A big ant hauls a small ant up a stick.
Do we call this fellowship or lunch? Let's say
the short guy mangled his paw on a tack
and his pal provides a kindly lift. Let's say

the shrimp has contracted a terminal ailment
and his buddy carts him everywhere tout de suite.
Back in real life the big ant lugs the small ant
into an ant restaurant. I brought my own steak,

he says. Make sure you cook it right! How cynical!
comes the anticipated complaint. But how quaint
is our human perspective. Isn't it possible

that all these fabrications are correct? Can't
we envy a full life cracking ant jokes and when
we die we're served as supper for our friends?

BACK TO SCHOOL

It just keeps getting better, brags the billboard
above the highway: an advertisement for a bank,
as if life were a balloon growing bigger
with no big bang in its future, a sense
of constant expansion, constant increase.
But listen, just as a ball hurled into the air
can reach the limit of its arc and plummet back
to earth, let's imagine that the forward motion
of humankind can falter, fumble, come to a halt,
then start shambling back again toward the sea.
The exec on the sidewalk in a three-piece suit—
mark how his spine is no longer straight, how his
curved fingers dangle at a level with his knees.
Like that primal fish who once ditched its pals
and swam off toward the sunlight, so our exec
turns on his heels and begins to seek out a cave
to squat in, a branch to swing from, a rock which
might conceal a food source. Why do we think
of always surging ahead, of eternal upgrade?
Bank accounts, intricate sporting events, sleek
bodies, meatless protein diets, high-tech gadgets—
perhaps instead of increase, these show decrease,
perhaps the arc has been passed and we're plummeting
back like a rocket tumbling to earth. Is it over
already? you say, as if we were the only creature
on the planet. But here comes the dog, eagerly
padding forward, still hoping to learn how to read.
What shaggy Shakespeares will the poodle produce?
And the snake slithering up its slippery slope,
what serpentine Leonardos lie ahead? And the ants,

how they love to march. Perhaps they are the ones
to construct a spaceship and populate the stars.
As for us, we've had our shot. Retirement now
is where it's at. With our new gills we won't quite
be sunning ourselves on a sandy beach, but near enough.
We're being sent back to school in the warm shoals;
a working vacation within the sea. Perhaps we'll learn
what went wrong, useful data for our data bank,
in case we're called upon to do it all again.
And won't we be eager? Won't we still maintain
it's not just hope but humankind that lasts forever?

BEAD CURTAIN

Sometimes late in the evening, I count the hairs
on the back of my hand. There aren't many, two
hundred or so. In the locker room, I see men
who are nearly fur covered, but I am blond,
or I was long ago. I like how the word hirsute
even suggests a suit of hair: a kangaroo tuxedo

or lion skin cape. If this is simple Darwinism
then perhaps I'm lucky not to have a few mackerel
scales as well, although maybe that occasional
eczema on my elbow suggests otherwise. I've done
pretty well: books published, a professorship,
a family I love that accommodates my eccentricity.

But these hairs on my hand—at night if I stare
at them long enough I seem to hear a distant howling,
then a shiver passes through all my property,
the expensive stereo system, the house itself.
I surround myself with images of substantiality.
These books, couches, all this music—someone else

will inherit, just as my few antiques have already
passed through a dozen hands—skeletal hands today
if even that. What does it mean to be substantial?
Do you remember those bead curtains that hung
in doorways in certain movies from the fifties? How
they quivered when someone walked through them.

These images of substantiality are no more solid
than that. This is when I count the hairs on my hand.

This is when I hear the howling. What a delicate
dwelling we have built for ourselves, yet how secure
we feel within it. For example, I love my motorcycle
but now at fifty-three I hesitate to ride it.

Even at the highest speeds one feels in control,
like a cockroach aloft on an arrow. I've thought
of shaving my hands, making them as smooth as a baby's,
but then what would I do for reminders? That arrow,
or thrown mud ball, or penny tossed from the top
of the World Trade Center, there must be tiny organisms

clinging to it that feel secure. Yesterday a friend
called from L.A. after the earthquake. We were lucky,
he said, we only lost two wineglasses—a neighbor
lost his house. These hairs on my hand, it's not just
the chaos in the distance they remind me of, but also
the chaos within, the chance of overthrowing my life

at any moment for a pretty face or from an eruption
of rage. What I love about complacency is that it tries
to make both past and future irrelevant by closing
the eyes to any possible threat: no earthquakes,
no meteors, no unexpected love affairs, nothing creeping
out of the past to grab my ankle. Opinions function

the same way—this can't happen, that won't happen
for the following best reason. But look at that
bead curtain, do you see how it trembles? So what
is the alternative? Should I think myself adrift
on an ice floe with a polar bear in the mood for lunch?
If so, then why get out of bed? Why take my head

from under the pillow? Love and the hope of love,
friendship, books, the joy of art, good Scotch,
even the random sporting event—these constitute
the white cane that keeps us tapping forward into
the dark. What a fine balance between too much fear
and too much forgetting. Don't the hairs on my hand

help remind me of that? It is January. Three feet
of snow cover the backyard. Schools are closed.
Laughing, my daughter tugs on her red snowsuit.
She is nine. When I ask her about her future, her face
wrinkles in anticipation of pleasure—a marriage,
a career, children, a dog. She wants to be a dancer;

she wants to be a vet. It's as if she were far
from home in a car driving fast. Where she lives—
oh, way in the distance—is a white house with blue
shutters, maples in the yard. Maybe a collie dog,
maybe window boxes with red flowers. This place
is her future. When she shuts her eyes she sees it

as clearly as her own face. She knows she will
get there shortly. I listen to her happy chatter
while with one hand I rub the back of the other.
What is substantial? These tender yearnings?
The debris of a life? Nothing? The bead curtain
trembles as something invisible slides through it.

HEAVEN

In the Greek underworld, the Achaeans
and Trojans cluster together. Death sticks
them all in one spot, killer and victim,
saint and sinner. Side by side Achilles
and Hector crouch on the stones, their

quarrels done; soon their wives arrive,
even their sons. But it's a dreary place,
no better than a prison yard with the lights
turned low, the perpetual gloom of eternity.
No bird calls, no kids playing stickball

in the street. I expect the concept of Heaven
began with the rise of the middle class. For
don't they need good and bad neighborhoods,
hovels to leave and mansions to move into?
Oh, Hitler, says one of the Saved, he lives

over yonder. And he points to a row of tumble-
down shacks. The Greeks would have the Nazis
and Jews all heaped up together, not fighting
but not happy either, a bunch of folks waiting
for the hot lunch that will never be delivered.

Perhaps it's a mistake to think of the harp
as originating in Heaven, because when we
visit on a tourist junket one summer evening
we find the Saved rocking in wicker rockers
on the great veranda, while from somewhere

comes the sweetest music: *Motherless Child,*
Steal Away. We ask one of the middle-class dead,
who even after cremation wears his pinstripes
and Rolex. That racket? he gripes. That's just
the bad folks yowling down in Foggy Bottom.

INDIFFERENCE TO CONSEQUENCE

Blossoms like the fluted bells
of miniature horns, these white flowers
less than an inch across, interrupting
the grass between sidewalk and street—
is this what it means to be joyous?

Tiny yellow stamens echoing the sun;
delicate violet ribbing echoing the dark.
Who were they in another life?
Men and women who drew each moment
lovingly into their bodies, admitting

their weakness, offering it to the world.
Humility means no pushing and shoving,
to accept a place with all that lives.
Not much of that in you. You survive
by your elbows. Squatting down,

you touch their white flesh, filled
with light, open to the rain. You envy
the lives they must have had, fortunate
souls continuing in good fortune.
What does it mean to be joyous,

to transform one's frailty into flower?
But even that judgment must be wrong.
To you the image of weakness is a wolf
offering its neck to the pack. Such
sacrifice is beyond your comprehension.

Effortlessly these flowers bear the gifts
that remain to you a mystery. Think
of the boots that will crush them here,
trash cans and car tires yanked over the curb.
Even in life their death couldn't scare them.

Can't that be a definition of beauty:
an indifference to consequence,
an embrace of the darkest possibility?
Isn't the courage of their acceptance
greater than the courage of your denial?

White blossoms touched with purple,
their beauty persists in them still.
These lives are not yours. Be grateful
that they breathed. Push on, push on.
Roar your meager motor ever louder.

TRYING NOT TO BE CYNICAL

These early risers—the cardinal's tenacious alarm,
the mockingbird's artful imitation of the street—
how keen they are to get started. I think of them
alert all night on their perches awaiting the signal,
which is not dawn because they begin long before
the first hint of light. The way that sunflowers
ardently follow their master or how the Irish setter

next door always has its sneakers on: it's not
the immediate moment they embrace but all moments.
The forward-looking, the ever-eager, surely they
suffer setbacks but the next morning the cardinal
is out there once again with its pygmy trumpet blast,
not only broadcasting its breathing but its readiness
as if the day held too few minutes for all its plans.

Don't we know people who are equally forward-looking,
unable to stay in bed, rushing from one embrace
to the next, eternally excited by the unexciting?
But there I go again: too cynical. As a hand fits
within a glove, so the energetic fit within their day.
The foolish ones have foolish projects, the brilliant
forge the ladder up which humankind has climbed.

What joins them is their embrace of each waking hour,
their gusto for commotion, the joy of inhalation,
but how difficult for those others to whom the moment
is a burden. How can one assert the superfluity
of all life when the fervent and forward-looking
are rushing back and forth like a cheerful spider
wrapping a melancholic insect in sticky strands?

But it's not that, only the cynical think that;
rather the ardent find heat where others find winter.
How eager they must be after death to return again,
standing in line wherever the line forms, perhaps
on sunset's ruby cloud or a rainbow's optimistic arc.
Who would trudge forward without their nudging, these
Casanovas of the instant, these embracers of breathing?

It is not yet four a.m. and the cardinal begins its call:
a benign airhorn cutting across the backyard fences.
In a dozen bedrooms, eyeballs rotate toward alarm clocks:
a groan, a sigh and the head goes back beneath its pillow,
hoping to snag a few more dreams before the day thoughts
start their interminable charting of what comes next,
a card house of plans plausible only to the impassioned.

TO KEEP ONE'S TREASURE
PROTECTED

Within the lump of coal the flame lies hidden,
within its darkness hides the diamond's glory:
all unseen from without, it must be imagined—
the fire that heats the house, the wedding ring
sparkling with future promise. But what would be
the coal's choice if coal could be said to choose?

All day I have been trying to imagine the ones
who withhold themselves—arms folded across chests,
or hands buried deep in their pockets. The ones
who remain a few steps back from life, who feel
possessed of a treasure which they don't wish
to offer the world, as if they wore their smiles

on the insides of their faces. Is this an attempt
to save themselves for the truly important moment?
Or could it suggest the world isn't good enough?
Or are they trying to be complete in themselves—
both lover and loved, consumer and consumed,
as if one could be complete without the world?

What does it mean never to offer, not necessarily
to be selfish but never generous, as if afraid
to spill a valuable part of the self, something
not seen as golden until it is gone, as if Self
were a red bird that one squeezes in the hands
thwarting its wish to fly off into the pine trees?

Those withholders in the doorway, those lumps
of coal who flee the fire: to see a man slip
to the sidewalk without going to help, to know
a song and not sing it, to watch the hungry
get hungrier, the defeated continue their steady
collapse. Our bodies are coinage. Spend it. Fling

the coins upward, hear them jangle on the street.
What happens to the souls of the miserly?
A man creeps down to his basement at midnight,
digs a hole, unearths a box, unfastens a lock.
Inside, a little dust, a spider, two lumps of coal.
A sigh—isn't it like a scream turned inward?

``LIL' DARLIN'''

The radio station was a rip in the fabric
of night air and through it came this song,
like someone tiptoeing from pillow to pillow.
I lived near Detroit, the station transmitted
from Boston. Always it was past midnight

when we heard this theme, although I never
remembered its name. I had a black 1951
Chevrolet convertible with Powerglide.
I was seventeen and where we parked, this
girl and I, was one of those predeveloped

subdivisions, curving roads and one model home.
We would rest between necking and smoke.
And always there was this Boston station
with its theme: a thin man stepping across
lily pads, perhaps he carried an ebony cane,

perhaps he wore a top hat. Even as we smoked,
we continued to touch, our faces smeared
with each other, clothing scattered, the car's
interior steamy and smoke-filled. We heard
other songs—Sinatra covering the waterfront,

Miles Davis in Spain—but this big band theme
opened and closed the show, a soft-shoe across
rabbit fur rugs. I wish I could paint you a picture
of the stars we had in 1958: silver confetti.
I believe the sky has fewer now. It was fall

and we had a blanket—backs cold, bellies warm.
The days themselves were nails and broken glass:
even today I don't see what the fuss was about—
high school, adolescence, it wore me out—but
that song was like a message sent from the future.

Here it was all scrambled eggs, but up ahead
lay black velvet with a dapper figure sliding
across it, although I had no idea how to get there,
didn't know I only had to wait, that the future
is always shuffling toward us, as if the sweet

dancer in the mystery tune signified the future
itself gliding toward Detroit. That Chevrolet
has long since been crushed to a cube of metal,
the girl's a matron now, an older woman I might
see in a supermarket. But recently in a bar

I heard the same song on a jazz jukebox: Count
Basie and his orchestra playing "Lil' Darlin' "
and I dropped in quarter after quarter. No tears,
I don't like tears. It was as if the tune described
a thirty-year period between then and now—a time

packed with event, the births of my children,
the deaths of friends—music given physical shape,
the palpability of notes strung out in a gentle
promenade and one solitary strutter in a black tux
stepping from circle of light to circle of light.

Look now, he is almost at the edge of the stage,
almost to the black curtain, he lifts his ebony cane
with the silver knob and touches it to his hat brim.
What a smile he has, gentle and conspiratorial,
as behind him one by one the lights blink out.

NOUNS OF ASSEMBLAGE

Two scenes lie before us. In the first
is a huge glass case in which a buffalo
from the Old West sedately crops grass,
actually Astroturf. Despite our different
museum exposure, we have each observed this.

Two feet in front a prairie dog sits up
on its hind legs. The buffalo is at rest.
Few cares weigh upon its soul. Its head
is huge, the size of an armchair and one
might think the brain inside to be almost

as big but that would be mistaken. The brain
is the size of a pea and the rest is simply
padding to keep the brain from getting lost.
Our second scene takes us to the historic
plains of Nebraska. Here the buffalo extend

farther than the eye can see. A quick-footed
acrobat might travel fifty miles jumping
from back to back. These beasts also lower
their heads as they calmly nibble the grass:
dusty but good. If any has a thought, it is

Food source, food source, but articulated
very slowly—a thought like a tiny cloud
in an otherwise blue sky. Suddenly, one
buffalo topples to the ground. The others
mosey a little over to the left or right

thinking, if they could think, More grass
for us. Then another falls and another.
The Sharps buffalo rifle could knock one
of those bruisers off his pins from several
miles away, but what could be heard over

all that munching? Whenever one of the great
beasts feels a twinge of anxiety, it lifts
its mammoth head and looks across the fifty miles
of its brothers and sisters. Don't be silly,
it might say to itself as it moves to make use

of the grass patch of the newly deceased. This
returns us to our first scene with the buffalo
in a glass case. The quality of thought between
the dead and living buffalo is very slight—
the difference between a stagnant pool and one

that is barely moving. Was that the problem?
The prairie dog, if it could speak, would say not.
Look at the ancient Greeks and Egyptians,
the Romans and Persians. Pick your favorite
group. Aztecs or Hottentots. When one fell

and the others took notice, didn't they stifle
their fears with the thought, We are too numerous
to kill? The prairie dog watches the visitors
approach—differences in hair styles and speech,
differences in dress. Do you see how he appears

to stare at each? Quizzical—that's how he looks:
twinkling eyes and perky ears. Perhaps he asks, Hey,
how's the weather? Or, even better, To what peculiar
(pick your preferred noun of assemblage: gang,
horde, clamor, litter, swarm) do you belong?

BEST IN THE BUSINESS

The snapper seats his subjects on the couch:
the grieving father, two sons and a daughter.
Okay, he says, let's do it. Tell them now.

They live in a trailer, a rundown mobile home
near Pontiac. The older boy is six or seven.
The snapper seats them in a row on the couch.

For skill and gall, he excels all the others
as the top news photographer at either paper.
Okay, he says, let's do it. Tell them now.

When police beat phoned about the accident,
he bolted his lunch, drove straight from Detroit.
He fixes his lights, seats the kids on the couch.

Even the toughest reporters dispute his technique,
the good and bad of it, while praising his cheek,
like the day he told the father: Tell them now.

The wife, a waitress, was killed in a car wreck.
Her kids only know something awful took place.
The snapper seats his subjects on the couch.
Okay, he says, let's do it. Tell them now.

NOCTURNAL OBSTRUCTION

How late the night will sometimes stretch,
that long expanse—is it only an hour?—
that drags from four to five o'clock

when the world slides through the cracks
and out on the street the traffic goes slack.
Too late for drinking, too early for prayers.

It is hard to think of life going on somewhere:
in one part of the world the day is beginning,
in another a farmer tethers a mule in its stall.

The night has dealt you a deep hole, a detour
in its steady progression of hours and if you
went outside right now, you would find yourself

on different streets, unfriendly neighborhoods,
with people who haven't had your luck. In how
many dreams have you run down these streets

with their dusty light, the deep twilight
that never seems to fade, as thin faces appear
in windows, then feet clatter on the steps

and you see them hurrying out of the houses
around you. Aren't you glad to be in your bed
right now while these others are safely outside,

staring up at the windows where they imagine
you sleep? If you looked, you would see them
waiting near the bushes: faces of cobweb, faces

of crushed leaves. Better not think about it.
Better shut your eyes and flick your sleep switch.
You need to rest to get ready for the coming day

when the gloves will be drawn up over the claws
and once more the world will wear its makeup.
What a pretty face. You know she loves you.

Think of it: the two of you arm and arm,
you with a little cane, she with her harmonica,
strolling down roads bounded by golden wheat—

bluebirds, rainbows, the paraphernalia of dream,
and what lies around the corner? Isn't that
the question? Maybe a cushion, maybe a chasm.

WHAT THEY DO ALWAYS

At night, on a journey, to hear the waves break
and to think, this is what they do always.

GOTTFRIED BENN

Through the Peugeot's open window we heard it:
the surf beating against the shingle.
On the curve, our headlights cut a triangle
of green across the eucalyptus. No other traffic.

Later, on the shore, we watched a distant light
far out on the ocean. It was easy to assume
it might be anything: men lost or returning home.
Moonlight whitened the froth jittering to our feet.

We sat on a stone wall and drank pisco in the dark.
All month my heart beat fast or slow, never regularly.
Hearing the surf, I heard my heart listening as well.
It beat evenly now. Who said it couldn't be taught?

A mound of stones, a shrine for a fisherman drowned
at age nineteen. Inside, a candle stub still flared.
At high tide the waves approached within a few yards:
fingers reaching toward what would never be found.

Waking in the dark, I felt I had misplaced myself,
then I touched your bare skin. The wind blustered.
The tide rushed in across the sand and retreated
in a sigh. Tell me why I can't translate that tongue.

Daybreak, the sun crept over the hilltop to calm
the rough water. Did it feel solace? I felt solace.
From nearby a smell of coffee. The orderly trespass
of the waves and my breathing came in unison.

In bed tonight, miles inland and half a world away,
I listen to my blood pulse as my head rests on my arm.
I hear the beats as if hearing the surf. I maintain
I am someplace, that it only resembles no place.

As the waves fell back, a line of sandpipers sought
the edge of froth as if trying to thread a needle.
The crimson flame of sunset shone on each ripple.
I must repeat to myself: this happens every night!

My students are mute, my daughters fight, my friends
full of complaint, my heart's a bag of chipped bone.
A pelican halts in its arc, drops like a rock. From
here a splash makes no sound. It must be imagined.

SKETCHING HECTOR'S EYE

In my sketchbook of Lonely Moments
there is a figure I draw especially
sustaining, at least for today, for I keep
the book to ponder what other folks do
when life doles out a cul de sac. Think
of those occasions at four a.m. A lot
of philosophy gets mulled over at that hour.
Or when your lover walked out, a parent died,
you lost your job—and we all know worse
unthinkables than these. Isn't this why
we read? What did the other guy do?
It's all about the future, right? That pitch-
black room into which we feel our way.
So today I sketch Hector. He has stopped
his panic-stricken flight from Achilles
because his brother Deiphobus has joined him
and together they hope to beat the big guy.
Achilles hurls his spear and misses, which
encourages Hector, makes him think that life
is looking up. But don't we make the same mistake—
cheered by evidence and all of it false?
Because it's a hoax. That's not Hector's brother
but the goddess Athena who hates Hector and when
Achilles hurls his spear, she nicely returns it.
Hector, still hopeful, throws his spear and misses.
Then he turns to his brother. Quick, he says,
give me another. But the man is no longer there.
One of those short moments that feels like
a long moment, a moment like a vast white wall
and Hector occupies a minuscule speck upon it,

as if all that space were knowledge. Because
doesn't loneliness depend on understanding?
And in that moment Hector understands it all,
sees that he is a figure in Achilles' story,
rather than Achilles being a figure in his.
Clear-sightedness, that was Hector's gift.
But just when most might sit down and lament,
Hector raises his sword and rushes forward.
And isn't it beside the point that Achilles
promptly kills him with a chop to the neck?
So this is how I draw him, raising his sword
and rushing ahead. Certainly it is clumsy
and I must do it over and over. How else can I
catch that look of panic posing as insolence.
Really, the picture doesn't show Hector's body
but his eye, which I sketch trying to locate
courage where there is terror, apparent
fearlessness in the face of certain death.
If I do it daily, then perhaps I'll get it right,
improve it to the point where I can cut it out
and stick it to my face when my own time comes,
to use instead of the look I possess, the one
showing only a wish to run and hide, to cringe
on my knees and weep as my own story ends.

COLD MARBLE

These poppies with their heavy heads,
how fragile is their beauty. The wind
knocks them casually to the ground,
a single hard rain will break them.

The weight of their petals, the elements
which attract us, also cause their ruin.
I think of beautiful women I have known,
how few had the strength for their beauty,

how it became a burden, something which
entered the room before they themselves
seemed to enter, meaning it was always
put first, seemed to exclude them, even

betray them, like finding one's best friend
in the arms of an enemy. Or that whore leaning
against a wall in a parking lot in New York,
a face like a Bellini madonna: she catches

my eye. Want it, she says, do you want it?
As if her beauty were the stranger with whom
she was forced to live. Another woman
who slashed her face, the one who drank,

a third woman who covered her blond hair
with ugly scarves—they hated being second,
of arriving on stage after their beauty,
after the buying and selling was done.

One would think the poppy's beauty
would be its blessing as it is for us,
but for the beautiful how often they hate
how their beauty denies them a life,

as if their beauty were a younger sibling
they had to take care of—has it eaten,
is it properly dressed?—until it becomes
the neuter pronoun. Coinage, cold marble—

truly not oneself; rather, the destroyer
of self. How strong must be the ones who bear
their beauty effortlessly and with grace.
Yet this morning after last night's storm,

I find the poppies sprawled in the dirt—
crimson petals, flesh-colored petals,
their black centers hidden—how relaxed
they seem in their destruction, as if glad

to be a memory. In the nursing home,
a woman over ninety gives her wrecked
cheek a friendly pat. Once this face,
she tells me, could break a man's legs.

STREET RACKET

I imagine a soul that returns to earth
must have a body. But is it necessary?
Hearing the motorcycles on the next street,

the growl of a dump truck, my neighbor's
cracked muffler, I think of the souls
of the scornful. Must they have shape?

Can't the scornful persist as traffic's
harsh vibrato, a motor's flatulence?
And what of the object of their protest?

One assumes the insult came first and scorn
rose up to fight it, but perhaps the object
came second. Perhaps scorn came first

and went in search of a victim. Jews or jazz
or short people—each person or thing has someone
to despise its being. The victims don't matter,

the victims come after. What the scornful
possess is a certain stance, a ready response
that defines them—the curled lip, arched

eyebrow—that existed before it found out
what it needed to be scornful about.
Where does it come from, this hunger

to measure and compare, this itch to divide,
to demand a special place? Could they be
born like this? I don't believe it. What

touched them as children? To deny one thing
is to affirm another. Isn't their scorn
an attempt to assert the truth of whatever

philosophy propels them? Aren't they trying
to affirm their own self-worth but failing?
Perhaps they think themselves unlovable

and so attack what seems less lovable than they—
tall people or blacks or rock and roll.
They work to persuade themselves it is okay

to love themselves. What happened to them
as children? What was withheld? Listen to them
on the street. How hoarse their voices have grown,

all language reduced to automotive racket.
These are the ones who felt poorly loved
and so found scorn. When they say *hate that,*

aren't they saying *love this?* At the curb,
our ears are filled with their complaint.
Can we imagine the lives they led and left behind?

How hard to love the world; we must love the world.

GARDEN BOUQUET

For today at least the snow has gone
and the backyard is awash with daffodils.
See how the sun has come to court you? Quick,
take a snapshot, just to remind yourself
when the weather skulks back to normal.

Between the sun and yellow flowers exists
a silent chatter as the daffodils push
through the matted leaves and detritus
of winter. You try to think the flowers
and blue sky offer an essential worth

beyond any you impose on them. Fragile stems,
frail blossoms: how muscular they must be
to bear your pleasure. For the cat they form
a decorative cover in her constant quest
for creatures small and briefly inattentive.

Across your eyes today is also a picture
from the paper: a man with a cigar and his legs
spread apart shooting his rifle at another man
collapsed on the ground. Nothing is special
about this photo. Yesterday had its picture;

tomorrow will have another. These scenes
are the tinted glasses that human beings
learn to look through. No wonder the flowers
seem fragile. Most days are neatly divided—
flowers on one side, violence on the other.

Too bad, you say, about the victims of Monday,
and you turn away to whatever you call pretty.
But today something has broken in your eyes.
Today across the daffodils and blue violets
sprawls the figure of Tuesday's corpse. This one

is Moslem, yesterday's was Texan or German.
Where can one go to get one's eyes fixed?
You would like to apologize to your wife
for the ugliness you have spread across
the flowers she has personally tended.

You have put blood on the blossoms and it won't
wash off. If beauty is a human valuation, then
is the ugliness of murder equally subjective?
This corpse between the flowers and your eyes,
perhaps it's wrong to think it wrong, just

as it is foolish to think the flowers beautiful.
Some days all the answers are bad ones.
Some days there is only the word Stop
and you try to make a wall of it, then
beat your head against it. But of course

nothing stops and it is foolish to think so.
There is only this constant on-goingness
until your own private light blinks out:
the cruel variety, the savage bouquet,
the world's victims interspersed with flowers.

ARTISTIC MATTERS

The little killer must have his own room
deep in the body. I imagine him tucked back
behind the ribs or buried in the neck.

The little killer doesn't need a lot of space.
His room is like a cockpit, a control room
jammed with chrome-plated switches. You would

like me to think you have no little killer.
That is because you wish to believe yourself
innocent. Otherwise you can't sleep, can't eat,

can't be happy. Relax. Maybe you won't need him.
Maybe his influence will continue to be discreet.
Tell me three characteristics of the little killer.

His eyes are the color of water; his hands keep
fiddling with the switches; there is nothing he loves.
Remember that baker in Berlin who butchered

those women? His little killer must have grown
terribly fat. People said, But he was always
so kind! They were silly to find a discrepancy.

But I shouldn't say Berlin as if the little killer
lived far away or was confined to history.
You would like to explain that your little killer

resembles your appendix. Although he may exist,
he has been unhooked from the rest of the system.
How sweet are your protests. They almost

make me like you. Let's say a team of doctors
searched the body for the little killer.
The doctors have a volunteer with a complicated

sense of guilt. They locate his little killer
and cut him out. But it's the old joke:
the operation worked but the patient croaked.

Does this suggest the little killer's secret spot?
His room of switches must surely be the heart.
But don't fret. Perhaps you will only perceive him

in how he looks at the world around you, but nothing
direct, nothing to upset your sense of indignation
or what you call justice, nothing to give bad dreams.

And what about your own little killer? you ask.
My little killer has a generous spirit. Although
hungry, he curbs his appetite. He transfers

his desire for blood into artistic matters:
loud music, garish pictures, offensive books.
You see? He has just written you this poem.

THE CASUALTIES OF APRIL

Man prefers to abandon life when it
is least difficult . . . when nature is
most smiling and the temperature mildest.
    ÉMILE DURKHEIM, Suicide

The first pulls a bag down over his head
and hopes to sing. The second uses a gun.
A third finds a high place. You think
he wants to fly? If he thought he
could do it, he wouldn't even try.
Oh, Dr. Durkheim, what are we to do?
When the tulips start to bloom we feel a little blue.

All winter he wrestled the darkness. As soon
as he reached warm weather, he knew it would
get better. More sunlight, more kindness,
more soft air stroking his skin. Of course
it didn't happen. The darkness grabbed him.
Oh, Dr. Durkheim, say it isn't so.
We find it easier to live when there's lots of snow.

Slambang, his dead self smacks the concrete.
We could have saved him, hung gloomy pictures
outside his windows, uprooted his roses,
honked our horns up and down his street. He
might have hung on. He might be going strong.
Oh, Dr. Durkheim, you know it isn't right
that when April rolls around a few give up the fight.

Let's ponder the problem logically. Sunny day:
bullet in the brain. Cloudy day: a little hope.
How hard to think rationally! Question: how are
soap bubbles, a bag of confetti and a human being
all similar? Answer: they blow as the wind blows.
Oh, Dr. Durkheim, we could have used your help.
It seems this task of living beats us to a pulp.

UNINVITED

Whose house calls cause you to crap on the floor?
Who makes you pee your pants? The Rude One.
For years you struggled to succeed, you combed
your hair and prayed at night. The Rude One doesn't care.
Your wish to buy a big TV, to summer in Nantucket—
the Rude One overturns your plans, upsets your spouse,
even the dog feels a loss. You were off to purchase
a new beret. Silly, no one wears a hat in a casket.

Think of it as a party. You have chosen the guests
except this boney one. But isn't he the loudest?
Isn't his dance the wildest? He brings his own jazz,
brings his own booze. The other guests are aghast,
but you must be entranced, seduced, enthused, because when
you bid adieu who has you on his arm? The Rude One.

FADE OUT

This one keeps the local liquor store,
that one runs the cleaners, this one owns
the news and smoke shop and chitchats
with his neighbors. These are the old guys
adrift in their sixties. Bad breath, bad teeth—
gray for them is like a hometown. I love
their mixture of impatience and humility,
the confusion of someone slapped around
by something bigger. I love how their eyes
rest on the vacancy of middle distance
and what they see there: the lottery lost
by one number, how they bought high
when they meant to buy low, all those
missed right turns when they took left turns.
Look at the seats they have made for themselves
behind their counters, the rickety chairs
with foam rubber pushing from the cushions,
their small offices with the radio always on,
the braided rug with an elderly Airedale or beagle,
the stale smell of unemptied ashtrays, maybe
an old *Sports Illustrated*, maybe a *Playboy*.
These places are like the hideouts they constructed
as kids: secret oaths and vows to stick together.
Now nobody is left to whistle them home.
Those gouges and wrinkles and creases—
it's not sadness that has carved up their faces
as much as surprise. Are these their lives?
Surprise at the streets, surprise at the papers.
Surprise at where they find themselves.
But I love how they fight their resentment,

how they keep moving their feet, how they
answer the question of How's it going with
Not bad, I'm breathing, It could be worse;
even though they know there's nothing nice
in their futures, nothing sustaining.
Then at night they lock up their shops
and the clouds press closer than ever
and the sidewalks to their nearby houses
are full of cracks and the dark seems one day
darker, their feet a little heavier. But they
don't stop, these guys with their professional
shrugs. They push forward up the front walks
of their small houses where the bricks need
pointing up, the clapboard needs paint. There
they pause before going in for the night.
They look at the trees and disappearing sky.
What are their thoughts? All the ways
it might have been, all the ways it is. But
no complaints, no whining, just another look,
one more cigarette before the door snaps shut.

HOMERIC OFFERING

Achilles leans back and strums his harp.
He wears something soft. The tent is warm
and rich carpets cover the dirt floor.

Do not trust this scene. Homer is again
displaying his sense of symmetry: murder
on one side, music on the other. The harp

comes from a town Achilles has sacked,
the songs he sings are songs of slaughter.
This is a scene of Achilles having fun

away from the battlefield. It shows
he wasn't an ox like Ajax, or a conniver
like Odysseus, or arrogant like Agamemnon.

Achilles is as nicely balanced as the world
that Homer places upon his shield, where
the good and bad are intermingled, the lion

and shepherd, the wedding scene and blood-price
paid by the killer, all the honey and uncertainty.
But what comes first? Doesn't Homer argue

that man must murder, no solving that, but
he can also be taught to play the harp and sing?
This makes murder the foundation upon which

the entire structure rests, a pleasing glass
palace set upon a dungeon. But if you get shot,
do you care if your killer also plays the lute?

Does it matter if he is handsome? To tell the truth
I'm glad when Paris nicks him with an arrow
and Achilles winds up with a mouthful of dirt.

Once in Hades Achilles seems to repent. "I'd rather
plough the earth for another, to be someone
without land and little to live on, than to rule

over all the dead." Or so he tells Odysseus.
Perhaps Achilles hopes a kindly god is listening.
Perhaps he hopes to regain his life by promising

to stop the killing. He will be good, read books,
go fishing. Even a lemon is sweeter than nothing.
Is this our only option: to gild the murderer?

Foresight—that's the faculty we humans lack,
blind action followed by tardy recognition.
But you see, argues Homer, he also plays the harp.

Tell that to his victims. How would they react?

DIGGING THE KNIFE DEEPER

One crystal of salt on the tongue. It isn't hot,
it doesn't burn, but it wants to dig a little hole.
We call it pleasing. Two poisons joined to make

a necessary taste. Let's expand that feeling.
Imagine a mouthful of salt, how it sucks water
from the skin, how it turns the skin to leather,

how it devours as envy devours. Your worst pal
gets the prize you coveted. Is not your mouth
full of salt? Those people more favored than you—

taller, smarter, more handsome, richer than you—
don't they chip away at your comfort? To be envious
is to let the world intrude too far, to be ground

by the world's gossip: he bought this, she won that.
Just as a field flooded by saltwater will no longer
produce crops, so the envious become barren. What

can they do but dig at themselves? If they can't
gain their heart's desire and beat their enemies,
then their only hope is to forget. But the world

loves to flaunt its merchandise; the big prizes
are always put on stage; the sexy and successful
like to assault our eyes. To forget means to retreat,

to reduce oneself, to turn one's back to the world,
turn the hatred inward (she bought this, he won that),
to turn one's envy into these sharp white crystals

that tear the skin and make one's ripped flesh burn
until the body twists like a snake tossed upon a fire.
And what is our response to the envious? Don't we

take pleasure in their predicament? Doesn't proof
of their distress form part of our delight? At least
this time it isn't us. We sit at dinner. A few grains

of salt between our fingers, to sprinkle on our meat
or place lightly on the tongue, minuscule fragments
of their complaint to make our evening more complete.

NO HANDS

Punch in the nose, kick in the head—
what is this explosion of the body,
this flowering of the physical that lets

the violent leave the world of courtesy
so far behind? It isn't anger. Anger
is the pretext; rather, a barrier

has broken, as on windy nights in spring
when we sit with friends and suddenly
the side door bursts open and the storm

invades the room, snuffing the candles,
hurling napkins and papers to the floor.
Kick in the belly, punch in the mouth:

as if the mind and body when tranquil
were a tightly closed bud which violence
unloosens to the hibiscus's red flower,

as if this flowering were the body's aim
and the violent themselves become victims,
surprised by their own overwhelming,

though surely less wounded than the one
who receives the whack in the teeth. How
could the souls of the violent have shape?

The men who like to kill or mutilate,
the women who like to break. What pleasure
must exist in destruction. Those photos

of Serbian soldiers machine-gunning a crowd—
how they were laughing. Could the souls
of the violent be trusted with substance?

Even their rough breathing is a weapon.
Think how the wind sweeps around the trees
unable to grab hold but wreaking destruction.

Think of the violent as fragments of air,
tugging at your clothes, riffling the hair.
Could you trust them again with muscle? Given

such good fortune, how they would bludgeon!
They heave themselves and thrust themselves.
Could you ever trust them again with hands?

It is the beginning of May. The weather
is mild. The breeze shakes the yellow heads
of the daffodils, then passes away.

CONSOLATIONS OF WATER

Picking your way barefoot across the parking lot
to the beach your face contorts as your feet
press down hard on the rough points of stones—
jagged stones, dagger stones, needles and knives.
Think of these as the souls of those who raged,
stripped of everything but hardness and sharpness.
Take one in your hand, feel its fierce condition.
This man struck his wife, the woman beat her son,
the boy punched his sister, she kicked the cat.
Rage, that breathless journey beyond the skin,
the past forgotten, the future wiped out.
Break it, smash it, all consequences gone.
Rage, its embrace becomes a style of flying,
escape from the body, escape from the heart.
Who are these harsh souls scattered around you?
Anger for them was a room to feel alone in.
Blows like oarstrokes as if they strove to pull
free of the planet, the tug of gravity, to flee
the sandbags hung by fishhooks from their skin.
Anger for them was a place to feel weightless in,
to be released from the world's grasp, the body's
ownership, to be unclasped and unencumbered.
But the world loves its little joke, to take those
who yearn to be air and squeeze them smaller,
to compact them into blocks of anger, to carve
their carcasses into emblems of their complaint.
Granite and glass, granite and glass. Can't we
forgive them? The world forgives them. See how
the waves stroke the beach, how the water's
soft hands seek to rub anger from stones.

BAD LUCK FENCE

Three jerks crack jokes on TV
while on the sofa a fat boy
snacks on chocolate. Outside,

the night hunkers over his house
like a walnut shell over a pea.
Maybe someone's about to get lucky,

but nobody out there likes the fat boy
and the fat boy likes nothing at all,
except the black flower which

he asserts will someday sprout
from his own sore prick. He will
water it and bring it honeybees.

It will shoot straight up a hundred feet
and prowl the streets to the spooky
music of monster flicks. It will bust

the big kids' bikes and won't take out
the trash for nobody. It will be his pal
but never ever get him in dutch.

Maybe it will bring him girls.
On the TV one comic quips about the creep
with inflatable ears. Whenever

he got a smart idea he half whacked
himself to death. Just like me,
thinks the fat boy, but I'm going

no place but Thursday. Down the street
at the cocktail lounge, the fat boy's
mother dabs on some color and smacks

her high-tech lips. Tonight's
her husband's bowling night and
who knows what might bring her luck.

With the right smile she might slip
some Romeo a smooch: a tap-dancer to jazz up
the doleful two-step of her life.

Meanwhile, as far as bowling is concerned,
her husband has spent the night
in the gutter. No luck for me, he thinks,

I might as well get drunk. Luck for him
takes place in other folks' stories.
Like the Japanese, it lives over the ocean.

Like the moon, it dangles above in the dark.
Mom, Dad and fat boy watch three separate TVs
where a comic jokes about the lunatic

accident victim struck by a psychosomatic
Mack truck. It could be worse, they think,
he might have lived. And a singer croons,

Every yesterday is the ghost of tomorrow.
Every tomorrow is the tombstone of today.
Every today is the cadaver of our dreams.

I'll drink to that, say Mom and Dad.
If they weren't so filled with hate
they might make a date to fornicate.

Three citizens who should be dearest chums,
why is each the enemy of the other?
What poison spoils their lives?

On this long night who will pluck them
from their bad luck fence, who will guide them
to the river and cleanse their wounds?

And the fat boy croons to his chocolate,
Oh, black flower, black flower
come put me in your power.

HANS IRONFOOT ET AL.

Today we visit Last Stop Castle in Dead End
Land and all the Instamatic cameras flash
as the prince and his bride incite the crowd

to rapture. This young man took top prize
in a perilous quiz, and the princess and half
her father's kingdom was his reward. How

tedious! The daily grind of champagne corks
and white cake spoils the soul, distracts
from the mysterious black door at the start

and finish of life's journey. But let's inspect
the opposite part of town, now seldom visited,
where the official axe-man did his work.

See that mound of two hundred grinning heads?
These are the guys who got the questions wrong,
the ones who always failed at riddles, the ones

who fell asleep too often. These are the sons
who won't be coming home, brief footnotes
in future genealogies, e.g. Hans Ironfoot strayed

into a forest of brambles and never seen again.
Even in death they keep their hopeful expressions.
Please, Sir, may I hear the question one more time?

But how hopeful could they have truly been?
Orphans and grade school dropouts, the sons
no one needed, who had already flunked

Sword Play and Dragon Dumping One-Oh-One:
these were the dreamers, the moon-watchers,
and a smart idea in their soft heads would drift

like a leaf down a stream. They heard a story
of a princess in a coma, or a princess trapped
in a glass tower, and they scratched their brows

and thought, Maybe I'd have a chance at that.
But what must first have gone already wrong
for them to have risked their necks in a series

of trick questions: when is a fly not a fly, what
lies beyond the blue door, what is the square root
of a zebra? Without doubt they realized this was

their last shot. What ruin set them to such odds?
And when one by one they laid their heads
on the executioner's block, it must have been

almost with a sigh of relief. No more pushing
and shoving, no more coming in last. Is this
why their skulls are grinning? And the prince,

the one who got the question right, who never
made a mistake, the valedictorian of his class—
his name is Jack and he is one dull boy. Even so

the cheering crowd is joyfully awash in a waterfall
of praise. They see in Jack everything they lack
and in the mound of heads everything they are.

But let's get our priorities straight. Hans
Ironfoot, Ivan Brokensnout, Morgan Potlicker—
these optimistic losers are our brothers.

Let's free their heads from the fly-encrusted pile
and bury them all in an enigmatic hook and dot,
each with a rose bush on top so when they bloom

they form a giant question mark seen from the sky.
The failed riddle, the philosophic shrug and the whack
of the executioner's axe—these make up our emblems.

The muddy road veering off into the dark woods,
the tattered boots, thickening gloom, the horror
around the further corner—this is our future.

We are the slapped look of surprise between
a pair of question mark ears, the cheese slice
in a mystery sandwich. On top of our family tree

a monkey diddles himself and cracks his lice.
Let's hoist this severed head in both our hands,
brush the worms from its lips and plant one fat

sloppy kiss. It's long overdue and just for you.

SANTIAGO: PLAZA DE ARMAS

As the lark hates the snake, so is salt
antithetical to sugar and so does the dark
despise the light. Consequently, how sweet
is the alert affection the pickpockets bear
for the Evangelists who gather in the square
with their guitars and singing and white shirts,
their upraised Bibles and praise of *El Señor*.
And like luscious peaches ripening on a branch
people just off work turn toward the music
which if lively draws a tightly packed crowd.
The infectious vitality and heartfelt singing—
this is when the plump fruit reaches its peak,
and pickpockets praise a dark lord of their own
as they stroll among the heavily laden boughs.

LET'S TAKE A BREAK

Recently in dreams I keep being late
for trains or caught without clothes. Maybe
I'm wearing just a bow tie or pink sock. Maybe
a single shoe. Yes, yes, I've grasped what

it means: precise night notes to the self about
vulnerability, anxiety and the rising tide
of chaos, like roller-skating down the side
of the Statue of Liberty's nose. Let's not forget

Nietzsche after his brain popped, scratching his head
and repeating: I am dead because I am
stupid, I am stupid because I am dead.

Let's take a break. Let's exit to some exotic land
where fat mice snooze beneath sombreros and at sundown
owls swoop from the palm trees crying: *¿Quién, quién?*

THELONIOUS MONK

A record store on Wabash was where
I bought my first album. I was a freshman
in college and played the record in my room

over and over. I was caught by how he took
the musical phrase and seemed to find a new
way out, the next note was never the note

you thought would turn up and yet seemed
correct. Surprise in 'Round Midnight
or Sweet and Lovely. I bought the album

for Mulligan but stayed for Monk. I was
eighteen and between my present and future
was a wall so big that not even sunlight

crossed over. I felt surrounded by all
I couldn't do, as if my hopes to write,
to love, to have children, even to exist

with slight contentment were like ghosts
with the faces found on Japanese masks:
sheer mockery! I would sit on the carpet

and listen to Monk twist the scale into kinks
and curlicues. The gooseneck lamp on my desk
had a blue bulb which I thought artistic and

tinted the stacks of unread books: if Thomas
Mann depressed me, Freud depressed me more.
It seemed that Monk played with sticks attached

to his fingertips as he careened through the tune,
counting unlike any metronome. He was exotic,
his playing was hypnotic. I wish I could say

that hearing him, I grabbed my pack and soldiered
forward. Not quite. It was the surprise I liked,
the discordance and fretful change of beat,

as in *Straight No Chaser*, where he hammers together
a papier-mâché skyscraper, then pops seagulls
with golf balls. Racket, racket, but all of it

music. What Monk banged out was the conviction
of innumerable directions. Years later
I felt he'd been blueprint, map and education:

no streets, we bushwhacked through the underbrush;
not timid, why open your mouth if not to shout?
not scared, the only road lay straight in front;

not polite, the notes themselves were sneak attacks;
not quiet—look, can't you see the sky will soon
collapse and we must keep dancing till it cracks?

for Michael Thomas

ODYSSEUS DISCUSSES ACHILLES

See him there, standing by the shore,
leaning on a spear driven into the sand.
You might think he is brooding;

he is waiting. His vanity is a lily
when its petals curl and wither.
It needs water. Without him, of course,

we might lose the battle. Without him,
success depends on each man's courage
and constant effort: plain human skills.

But when Achilles fights, he is the wind.
He is terror loosed from its container.
The world has no corner from which he cannot

chop himself free. And between battles?
Briseis was the lover of his vanity,
Patroclus the lover of his body, but only

Death embraces his whole self and Achilles
simpers, flirts, attempts to seduce it.
All else he loves is less than this love.

Do you see why many hate him? He has
gone past the human. He calls it godlike.
Is that what it means to be a monster?

He is without moderation. As for us,
where would we be without our dream
of a homeland, of friends who love us?

Those dreams are the citadel which
we may not surrender. To give them up,
isn't that to forfeit our very souls,

as Achilles has lost his soul? What is
a sense of limit but a sense of love?
Tomorrow when Paris brings him down

with an arrow to his ankle, his one
vulnerable spot, it will be argued
that a god directed the shot. Not true.

The Trojans prayed for such good news.
We gave it gladly. Far simpler
to have Achilles' example erased

than to have us forget the softness
of our own flesh as we let him lead us
in attack after attack. Like Patroclus

he will have a fine funeral to show off
our homage and respect, the only gift
we can give a monster—slaughtered cattle,

slaughtered young men and Achilles himself:
black smoke rising into blue sky,
irreconcilables which the wind disperses.

WHO IS MISTAKEN?

These small lizards darting across the white
stone wall to hide beneath an ivy leaf,
they resemble the curve of an eye, the arch
of an eyebrow, an escaped question mark—

see their delicate matchstick feet, these
nearly transparent souls, not trusting themselves
to the physical, like someone in a doorway
with darkness on one side, sunlight on the other

and afraid of trusting himself to either. Perhaps
they were like this on earth, the timorous ones.
The lizard darts from leaf to leaf. Is anxiety
a defense or a philosophy? Can one exist

in acts of self-negation? The shy, the timid:
does one preach the lie that no one will
do them harm? Here in the garden the gray cat
waits to snatch the lizards off the wall.

So it is with the world. Is it destruction
that the timid fear? Or do they only avoid
interruption as they seek to knit the scattered
threads of their being into solid cloth? Do they

dream in another world and only their bodies
stay among us? Is this why they seem distracted?
They scuttle from spot to spot, their speed
and skill at concealment their only defense.

We would like to convince them it is safe here
but it is not the timid who are mistaken,
we only want them to be mistaken. Perhaps this
is the lie they exist to reveal to us. We want

a world in which the cat doesn't wait. What
does it mean to be safe? These lizards remind us
of our desire and our dream. They represent
one half of our nature. And the other? See

the cat's pleasure as he snatches the lizards
from the wall, these timid souls through which
the light burns. How pleased he is with his
brute nature. Some he plays with, some he eats.

for Margot Balboni

PINK SPOT

The noisy fat girls next door are busting
the seams of their kiddie bikinis as they
splash in their plastic pool. If any exists
at all, it is at the apex of her shriek.
They are slabs of white cake brought back
to life—too much sugar, too much grease.
Consider their existence on the glass shelves
of display cases—the purple bouquets and pink
filigree of frosting duplicating the needle tips
of their squeals. These are the girls who clogged
my father's heart, the human equivalent
of cholesterol, until a surgeon equipped him
with new arteries cut from his leg which he soon
choked again with white cake. Had he been
a neighbor to their clamor he might still
be living, absorbing their grease and sugar
safely through his ear. Their racket packs
my intellect and wrecks my logic. Let's take
a moment to reflect on their erratic makeup.

Souls like theirs one sees at carnivals
where latex gives a shape to their screeching,
their yelps of delight filling holiday balloons:
helium-packed bunnies with shell-shocked eyes,
yellow duckies with kissable beaks. Vocal, playful,
cheerful, but as undependable as ever. See that
child by the popcorn stand with the broken heart?
Nothing fills his veins but absence and he yowls.
Foolishly he released the treasured string
(he felt it loved him too much to flee).
Look up, look up! Do you see that pink spot?
One more noisy soul escaping back to heaven.

GOLDEN BROILERS

What is it about how these chickens set
their scrawny feet precisely in the dirt
that implies judgment? The measured step,
the upraised beak. Not all walking birds
have this trait, not the turkey, nor the duck—
a way of locomotion that suggests division
between one citizen and another, a partition
between the exalted and paltry. The souls
of the judgmental must take their comfort
in birds like these, must applaud their finicky
perambulation of the barnyard. What is this itch
to invoke valuation, to seek out verdicts?
The critic, the bureaucrat, the insecure
all crave a pointer with which to cause rupture.
This is lovely, this ugly. This moral, this bad.
To carve the world into a patchwork of value,
then pass laws to keep it like that. To create
a yardstick that swaps one's subjective groping
for objective truth. There are only six
great writers, says the famous poet. The finest
lyric voice since Keats, says the famous critic.
The chicken struts across the dirt, pecking
at the gravel, turning neither left, nor right—
data have been digested, rulings reached, decisions
declared. No other opinions will be heard. Don't
the judgmental work to veto every other voice?
They hope to be the only ones to hold the scales.
Are there no others? Five bucks, says the butcher,
as he slaps the chicken's carcass across the counter.

BEING HAPPY

A dog on a street corner sits on a soapbox
smoking a cigarette, a non-nicotine
version. In fact, he puffs talcum.
Nevertheless, the passersby are flummoxed.

From the dog's neck hangs a sign that states,
Ask the Wizard a question for two bits.
The dog is a black mutt with a white patch
circling his right eye. A Chock full o' Nuts

coffee can is stuck between his front paws.
People begin to line up. An aging spinster
drops in a quarter and asks, Will I ever
find happiness? The dog lifts his right paw,

meaning yes. The woman walks away beaming.
A man in a three-piece blue suit asks,
Am I truly envied? Again the dog hoists
his right paw. And this keeps happening

all morning. Does my lover love me?
Will my children someday support me? Will
I find a job into which to throw myself
body and soul? Will I publish my mystery?

Yes and yes again. The line of eager
askers winds around the corner. If streets
could express emotion these would smirk,
but nothing lewd, nor rude, nor superior,

even streets like to see folks being festive.
About lunchtime a ragged man wearing a Mets
baseball cap jogs up to the dog and asks,
Like some chow, Spot? Again the dog elevates

his right paw. The man dumps the coffee can
of coins into his bag, the dog stubs out
his cigarette and both seek out an Automat
where the dog can encounter a broad range

of choices: burgers and beans, kidneys
and cake. A newsboy bellows, You've all been
hoodwinked! In the world of fact, newsboys tend
to be correct. But in offices around the city

men and women are perking up. They ardently
anticipate hurrying home to their helpmates.
Even from this distance, tomorrow looks bright.
Weekend clambakes are planned. He's a phony!

shouts the newsboy. What difference does it make
if he's right? In the Automat, the ragged prankster
asks, Have some cheesecake, Spot? The dog hoists
his paw. Afterward, they tip the busboy five bucks.

for Carol Houck Smith

EDUCATION

The day I stepped back off the cabin porch
and fell, the crippled kid laughed and I
slapped him. For forty years my hand has
felt that blow. Till then we'd been friends.
His name was Spike. He had red hair
and lived in a whorehouse in Pittsburgh
with his grandmother and a bunch of aunts.

I was fifteen and a camp counselor. Spike
was fifteen and spastic. He could run but
he couldn't stop. One morning he ran out
on the dock and you could see his face
alter as he reached the end: pure terror.
He was fully dressed and couldn't swim.
Even in midair his legs kept churning.

Someone dragged him out. Many kids came
from even worse homes: the six-year-old
who pimped for his mother, the twelve-
year-old girls who tried to fuck counselors
for cigarettes, the sixteen-year-old black kid
with the cheap metal leg hung from his pelvis
where he kept his switchblade and skin magazines.

The leg squeaked and needed constant oiling
so the glossy tits of the girls were dolloped
with great greasy drops. The boy would swing
his hip to unhook the leg, grab his knife,
dripping with oil, then fall flat on his face.
Lying in the dirt, he'd laugh till he wept.
And this was just the surface damage—

incest, sexual abuse and constant beatings
was what kept them crying out at night,
till one envied the idiots with their constant
masturbation or the mongoloid singing one
nursery tune over and over or the bleeder
who would die soon. Spike, the red-headed kid,
would discuss his aunts and how they loved him.

Camp for him was just a nuisance. He wanted
to get home to the laughter and presents. Maybe
these kids were lucky to have their failings
so conspicuous. The counselors were supposedly
normal teenagers and college students: the bully,
the mean, the timid or vain, the sexually obsessed,
just regular people, half jailers, half protectors.

Each week on my day off I hitchhiked to town,
spent the night in a cheap hotel. The dirtiest book
on the drugstore rack was *Tom Jones* and I stayed
up late looking for the good parts. In such a way
did education start. Of course I felt myself superior.
Is one changed by time or does one change oneself?
By now the mongoloid who sang so prettily is dead,

others also. But what died as well were the visions
of the future, the foolish plans, of feeling better
than the rest, as when I fell off the porch
and Spike laughed and I slapped him, then watched
the mark of my hand on his cheek fading and with it
our friendship and my own good opinion of myself,
one more cripple, another tyrant among the rest.

THE INVITATIONS OVERHEAD

At the edge of a golf course, a man watches
geese land on a pond, the bottom of which
is spotted with white golf balls. It is October
and the geese pause in their long flight.

Honking and flapping at one another, they seem
to discuss their travels and the man thinks
how the world must look when viewed from above:
villages and cornfields, the autumn trees.

The man wonders how his own house must look
seen from the sky: the grass he has cut
a thousand times, the border of white flowers,
the house where he walks from room to room,

his children gone, his wife with her own life.
Although he knows the geese's honkings are only
crude warnings and greetings, the man also
imagines they tell the histories of the people

they travel over, their loneliness, the lives
of those who can't change their places, who
each year grow more isolated and desperate.
Is this what quickens his breathing when at night

the distant honking seems mixed with the light
of distant stars? Follow us, follow us, they call,
as if life could be made better by departure,
or if he were still young enough to think it so.

PRIMAVERA

He loves his wife and to her he gives this present:
a returnable bottle, dangling from a stick.
He is our brother, tricked by delusion and deceit.

Perched at the top of a Dumpster, he has spent
ten minutes fishing for a bottle worth five cents—
he loves his wife and to her he gives this present.

It's a balmy spring morning on West 14th Street
and the woman holds up her bag of black plastic—
she is our sister, tricked by sham and deceit.

As her husband maneuvers the stick with the string,
her eyebrows rise and fall, reflecting her excitement.
She loves the husband who offers her this present.

They are Mexican or Guatemalan, chubby and short,
dark skin, black hair, perfect Mestizo stereotypes,
who traveled north because they believed the deceit

of the ads, the TV shows, the promised junk
that seems to make a life complete. He wanted,
because he loves his wife, to give her this present:

an elegant life in New York, but he can't find work.
The emerald green bottle dangles from the stick.
The man loves his wife and to her he gives this present.
Our brother, our sister: victims of deceit.

THE IMPOSSIBLE

Now and then a Count Basie trio
will come to rest on a single note:
plink, plink, high up on the piano

and the world appears to pause
at the very vestibule of chaos,
as if in a twinkling all the notes

will go splat on the concrete and we
can only creep off to bed and weep.
How long it seems, those five or six

repeated notes, like a man on stilts
juggling a dozen cherry pies, and look,
here he is lifting one of his legs high

in the air. These stilts, maybe each
is twenty feet, and just when we think
he'll fall, he hoists the second stilt

and holds it—plink, plink—and we see
it's those damn pies holding him up like
a trapeze, and the lackluster newspaper

world retreats another quarter mile.
Then Louis Bellson hits the drums
to give us the ground again and Ray

Brown thrums us a road to run along,
and what was near chaos now is memory.
Did you check out that acrobat dangling

from a chain of cherry pies high in the air?
No answer. What is the impossible but
a fire ladder propped against a window

of a burning building where children sleep.
Shrieks and sirens. Feeling fretful? Don't.
Here come the kids safely scrambling down.

RATTLETRAP

Odysseus, when he is at last met in Book Five,
is weeping and full of complaint. At night he naps
with his queenly nymph and again begins to gripe.
All he wants is to go back to his homeland,
but when Calypso offers to help build a raft,
Odysseus suspects a trick, continues to grumble,
says the trip would be arduous and risky.

Much nicer to be sad with a luscious immortal
than to capsize in the Aegean. He won't be duped.
It's all a plot to make him shut up, until
even Calypso calls him naughty and is forced
to swear a great oath. Then Odysseus believes her,
but grudgingly. Isn't this the kind of hero
we like best, someone scared to death? And why

does he suspect a trick? Because he himself
is the master of deceit. Why fight if he can lie,
why lie if he can stab in the back. But maybe Homer
got the story wrong. Maybe Calypso didn't permit
Odysseus to depart, she probably kicked him out.
After all, what made him mortal also made him whine.
His complaints became his single favorite subject

and were he to receive the gift of immortality
he would be rendered speechless, since without
Death why should he open his trap? Perhaps that's
why any of us talk. If Sleep is the twin brother
of Death, isn't Silence at least a first cousin?
Consequently we jabber, not to communicate, but
to keep the motor running. Calypso no doubt had

gotten sick of the ruckus, so she let Odysseus
make a raft of twenty logs, add sails, barrels
of supplies and called a wind to set him traveling.
Soon the chatterbox was gone. It took three weeks
with gales and terrible trouble to make landfall.
Odysseus must have hollered the entire time,
as if Death hated to hear the human voice and fled

from any verbal racket. It must hurt Death's ears
as a high-pitched whistle hurts a hound's. Doesn't art
have this purpose as well? It pushes the darkness back,
because what seems to us symphonic must sound to Death
like breaking glass. Yet when Death cries out how sweet
must be its music. Years earlier when Odysseus heard
Death's voice drifting from the Island of the Sirens,

his one wish was to pass through its door to the green
land beyond. Luckily, he was tied to the mast, and once
his ship was out of range, he must have jabber, jabber,
jabbered, a hero like any other, preferring pleasure
to warfare, the hearth to the long march, a string
of witless jokes to drive disaster from the door,
the human whine that accompanies the long decline.

FLEAMARKET

A display of padlocks on a blanket on the sidewalk,
arranged as neatly as newborns in a hospital nursery—

I have known these souls, the ones who encourage
with a doorknob and frustrate with a key, who work

not to build something, but block something, the ones
who deny not from doubt or change of heart, but power,

the imposition of one muscle over another, men
and women who excite only to reject, that editor

who asked to read a friend's work, that teacher who
liked to tell students they were dumb, that shouter

who tried to shut down all other talk. A door
closes, a lock clicks, the division of space into

my space and other. Even in its shape, a padlock
duplicates the letters of the negative: the diagonal

imposed upon the zero. How hateful to be clustered
on a crowded blanket when each covets a single

blanket of its own. If you exist, then how can my
existence be of value? A locked room, a locked

soul, alone one can imagine one is anything:
a single multi-thorned rose, a window looking out

on the ocean, the embrace of the body by the body,
the eye that surveys the dark and sees only itself.

HOPELESS TOOLS

These thorns that snatch at our sleeves,
thorns of blackberry, thorns of rose,
brambles, thistles, burdock, cactus—
these are the souls of great desire,
the ones for whom a naked belly was a blow,
line of a breast, protrusion of a nipple—
images like broken glass beneath the eyelids.
What does it mean to hunger too much?
Where does desire turn to excess?
To be stunned by skin, the fat curve
of a lower lip, tight fabric outlining
a crotch, buttock making a ski slope
for the tongue. One may be making dinner
or brooding about Plato, one's mind may be
blissfully blank—when a sliver of flesh
can set all the wires jangling. What
does it mean, too much? These thorns
that tear at our clothes, scratch our skin
as we collect the blackberries, so juicy
and plump, is this not a hopeless yearning,
a useless attempt to possess, to hook
another self to one's flesh? How ferociously
they grab. They should be open mouths, open
sacks, open pits so that the world itself
can shovel life into their eager crevices.
Too late for that. The fires that burned them
have reduced them to ash. What lives after
are the tools they used to grab and hold on,
sharpness only, joy of tearing and rending.

ALLEGORICAL MATTERS

Let's say you are a man (some of you are)
and susceptible to the charms of women
(some of you must be) and you are sitting
on a park bench. (It is a sunny afternoon
in early May and the peonies are in flower.)
A beautiful woman approaches. (Clearly,
we each have his or her own idea of beauty
but let's say she is beautiful to all.) She smiles,
then removes her halter top, baring her breasts,
which you find yourself comparing to ripe fruit.
(Let's say you are an admirer of bare breasts.)
Gently she presses her breasts against your eyes
and forehead, moving them across your face.
You can't get over your good fortune. Eagerly,
you embrace her but then you learn the horror
because while her front is young and vital,
her back is rotting flesh which breaks away
in your fingers with a smell of decay. Here
we pause and invite in a trio of experts.
The first says, This is clearly a projection
of the author's sexual anxieties. The second says,
Such fantasies derive from the empowerment
of women and the author's fear of emasculation.
The third says, The author is manipulating sexual
stereotypes to achieve imaginative dominance
over the reader—basically, he must be a bully.
The author sits in front of the trio of experts.
He leans forward with his elbows on his knees.
He scratches his neck and looks at the floor
where a fat ant is dragging a crumb. He begins

to step on the ant but then he thinks: Better not.
The cool stares of the experts make him uneasy
and he would like to be elsewhere, perhaps home
with a book or taking a walk. My idea, he says,
concerned the seductive qualities of my country,
how it encourages us to engage in all fantasies,
how it lets us imagine we are lucky to be here,
how it creates the illusion of an eternal present.
But don't we become blind to the world around us?
Isn't what we see as progress just a delusion?
Isn't our country death and what it touches death?
The trio of experts begin to clear their throats.
They recross their legs and their chairs creak.
The author feels the weight of their disapproval.
But never mind, he says, Perhaps I'm mistaken;
let's forget I spoke. The author lowers his head.
He scratches under his arm and suppresses a belch.
He considers the difficulties of communication
and the ruthless necessities of art. Once again
he looks for the ant but it's gone. Lucky ant.
Next time he wouldn't let it escape so easily.

WHAT'S THAT, WHO'S THERE?

The shack was half a tube of corrugated zinc,
with great double doors hung across the front,
obviously an ex–body shop or garage.
Around it thousands of acres of Maine woods,
no other building in sight, hot August
afternoon. The hand-painted sign said,
Sophie's Redemption in red letters. You know
how your heart can catch in your throat?
Of course, I understood the sign meant
empty bottles and cans, but now the name
became fixed before my eyes: Sophie's
Redemption. How far the word had strayed!
What would it mean to start life fresh again?
What would it mean to be washed clean?
The car hardly slowed to sixty-five. But now
a sudden lack spread itself across the sky—
no one to care about my badness but the law.
No one to forgive me but my own cross voice
when I drag myself up to the bathroom at night—
So what? Let it go. Let that too slide by.
No way to get better but by personal hard labor.
It's a joke, right? How do you take an empty box
and make it emptier? Back in Vacationland again.
The trees gone bleak. My kids napping on the seats.
The great vacant world thrumming past my fenders.

ANCIENT TEACHING

As he makes his steady way across the planet
so he makes his way across his woman's body.
Isn't this what the ancients taught: as it is below
thus it is in the heavens? And so he charts
his life across her flesh and each sweet spot
where he lingers becomes a city he will roam
or a beach he will cast his body down upon,
a forest where he shelters from wind and sleet.

Without her, how could he journey anywhere?
Wouldn't he be like a blind man driven from home
with neither dog nor cane, stumbling over
rock after rock? But because of her he finds
each strange place familiar. He has been there,
he has tenderly surveyed her darkest corner.

SECOND SKIN

Your slick liquids coat my prick until I shower.
Why shower? My love, if we had never washed
in our sixteen years together, then the thick crust
with which we would be covered would be each other.
Like a pair of snapping turtles grown old together
we each would have a shell—those dried body juices
excreted by the other, our lover, a smelly house
in which to doze and dream of one another.

But to wash means always to begin afresh, to create
the blank page across which we scrawl our mark.
Clean, we mimic Alzheimer's patients stumbling along
an unknown path already toured a thousand times,
or better, with each new kiss we lip synch Armstrong
the Astronaut plonking his Astro-boot upon the moon.

THE BIG DIFFERENCE

Standing side by side on the stage are Pope
John Paul and Arkan the Serbian terrorist.
The Pope has saved ten million souls. Arkan
has ten thousand victims. But he's young,
he might catch up. Pope John Paul wears

clerical robes and carries a staff. Arkan
wears camouflage and holds a Kalashnikov.
They wave to the crowd, which is oddly restless.
Now four female assistants help the men undress.
Both are uncircumcised and have appendicitis scars.

The Pope is a little bowlegged, the terrorist
a trifle knock-kneed. We hear a dissatisfied
whispering from the crowd. The female assistants
push machinery onto the stage: X-ray apparatus
and CAT scanners. The two men receive intense

internal scrutiny. The results are shown on a screen.
Their lungs look about the same, although Arkan's
a smoker. Hearts, stomachs, livers and lights,
if we didn't know who owned what, we could easily
be confused. The crowd doesn't like this one bit.

Cut them up! shouts a man in back. Dissect them!
shouts another. We experience a tense moment, but
is it such a bad idea? Shouldn't their cells be viewed
beneath the microscope's shrewd eye? Ether is given,
surgeons appear, vats of ice, more machinery.

The surgeons start at the toes, cutting carefully,
nothing is permanently damaged. The crowd is tense.
Snips are made in their thighs, their bellies. Arkan
is a vegetarian, the Pope likes meat. Their hearts
each weigh two pounds. The crowd is on its feet.

A slice in the neck, their sinuses are scraped.
Their brains are held up for inspection. Each
is the same gray color and shape. The crowd pushes
toward the stage. Who is the saint and who the sinner?
One nurse, smarter than the rest, ducks beneath

Arkan's operating table and finds a spider happily
knitting its web in the dark. She removes it, then,
with a sleight of hand, appears to extract it
from Arkan's skull. We hear a universal sigh. Even
the surgeons feel better. Now comes the hard part,

the surgeons must stick the Pope and terrorist back
together. Didn't you label the parts? asks one. He
lifts a severed hand. I guess it must be done by guess.
Right ventricle, left ventricle, left brain, right brain.
The Pope has one brown eye and one blue, Arkan also.

After they recuperate, the Pope and Arkan go back
to the same work that kept them busy before the fuss—
salvation and butchery, Mass and murder—and everyone
is happy except the spider kept on exhibit in a box
in a museum with the label: Pure Evil. Check It Out.

STREET SMART

Just as the casual stroller comes to a street,
intending to jaywalk, and looks both ways
at the speeding cars, so the Greek gods came to time,
turning toward past and future with equal ease.

The big trucks rushing toward them out of tomorrow
were easily avoided; fire engines, ambulances—
the gods simply waited. As for us, we approach
time's busy boulevard only to find a one-way street

and we peer off in the wrong direction, as traffic
rushes toward us out of the other (our future),
and try to gather the data to decide when to leap.
Mostly the gods refuse to help us, even though

they may like us. Brave little tykes, they say,
as we jump in front of a speeding dump truck.
For our amusement, we have TV, even books.
For their amusement, the gods have us. And as we

can skip forward a few pages during a scary part,
so the gods know what is coming. So how touching
in *The Iliad* when Hector was deciding how to act
as Achilles dashed up to chop him into dog meat.

Should Hector fight, hightail it or maybe surrender?
The gods looked from their clouds and said, How cute,
because already they saw Hector dead in the dirt.
Our lives, those true-life dramas, which we take

so seriously, they watch as soap opera, or worse,
as Saturday morning cartoon shows, because what
immortality and the knack to look both ways
give the gods is deficiency. They need not change,

so do not change. Why fret? What can hurt them?
Only vanity and appetite propel them forward.
But consider the human creature waiting at time's
steep curb, calculating what has been, scrutinizing

the mercuric masses of mighty metal now departing
to gain an inkling about what might be approaching.
He sees periods of calm, periods of heavy traffic,
and reaches his decision, not always mistaken.

No doubt about it, the prospect of destruction
gives us a brain; the chance of a garbage truck
squashing our heads provides a real education.
And soon we resemble those street smart city kids,

dodging cars, snatching rides on the backs of buses,
while in gray stretch limousines with smoked windows
ride the gods, lounging lazily on tucked leather,
gazing at tiny TVs stuck into the backseats.

And what do they see on those miniature screens?
Why, they are watching us. They observe us jump
between two fat trucks and they say, How clever!
They see us crushed by a blue bus and say, How sad!

PUSHING AHEAD

A brushfire that sweeps up the hill devouring
the grass, chasing rabbits, baking the insects;
a forest fire leaping from maple to spruce,
whole valleys wiped out, villages threatened.

To grab something, to reach forward, to grab more,
to crawl through life hand over hand. The ambitious
eat and eat. What stomach is filled? What people
get tossed off behind? My neighbor tells me,

Each morning we had to have a six o'clock meeting.
Another says, It's just there for the taking.
To shove the world in one's mouth with both fists
while left behind are black scars, dead things.

Smoke rises, flames extend their rosy fingers.
To be ambitious means to possess all the space,
to become additional, to be always increased,
to be so engorged that one's past self resembles

a pebble seen from the top of a tall building,
an ant on a street corner. Who was I back then?
Someone with not enough room. The world squatted
on top of me, people jabbed me with their elbows.

Always I felt overlooked. People thought me
less than I was. I needed to separate myself.
My belly felt empty. I needed to make a fortress
of successes, a great barrier of merchandise.

First there was nothing, then came the spark,
then the yellow tongue licked out into the grass.
And isn't this sufficient space, this hillside
of charred tree trunks? I made it, this is mine.

GUTTER TROUBLE

Detritus in the roadway: broken bottles,
litter, scraps of paper in the gutter,
a Styrofoam cup blows across the street;
or these meager houses with chipped paint,
cracked glass, a patchwork of missing
shingles across their swayback roofs,

shapeless women in shapeless dresses,
kids running and screaming, a broken bike.
Does each object at birth have a purpose
or is there a choice of paths to follow?
Color of rust, color of gold—sometimes
only a shade or two may divide them.

This man drinking from a bottle tucked
in a paper bag—what mixture of ill-fortune,
poor choices and missed chances landed him
on a broken porch in a torn T-shirt? The lives
of the disappointed give off a smell like
rusty metal or a splash of vinegar, the odor

of the air after lightning or burning weeds
drifting over a backyard fence. Is it because
I have passed half a century that I keep
meeting people who speak of the downturning
of their lives: teachers at little colleges
who dreamt of big colleges, the childless,

the still unpublished, the deep in debt,
the loveless, no one to caress their cheeks?

Ambitions of the morning, desolations at night:
I thought by the age of fifty, I'd be rich;
I thought by the age of fifty to have a book;
I thought by the age of fifty to find someone

who truly loved me. What happened when they
looked the other way? What passed them by?
Let's say there is no purpose. We have only
different roads stretching away at birth.
How can we tell which path is the right one?
The cruel and disappointed, the barren and lost—

each one has a story. I had the greatest plans.
I had the best intentions. I had such aspirations.
I wanted ten children, ten happy children.
Broken bottles, splinters of wood, strips
of plastic, gravel, metal, scraps of paper—
I watch my neighbor rake it from the gutter.

No telling what these bits once were except
they were whole and had a purpose, horizons
far different than to be junked on a side street.
Sunlight glitters across broken shards of glass:
a man says, When I was younger my dreams of what
I hoped to write woke me from the soundest sleep.

VISITOR

Those patches of cold air on the far side
of the barn at night or down the hill
among the trees—what souls are these?

What must have happened for them to linger
as such tentative gestures—the touch
of damp air against the skin, the smell

of wet stones in rain? What disappointments
induced them to deny all shape? The chill air
of cathedrals, train platforms, the stairwells

of office buildings—is this where they gather,
taking solace from human company without
the burden of substance? Men and women

who spent their lives behind closed doors,
who listened to footsteps on the street,
who burned one candle, owned one spoon,

who slept in beds as narrow as coffins.
In some persisted the image of a face,
one who passed by and never looked back.

Others were denied even that and sailed
toward death like ships empty of cargo.
Men and women so soft-spoken that even

their affirmations were denials, these
self-effacers, drawing a line with one hand,
erasing it with the other. What could have

raised their voices, coaxed them forward?
How difficult to say, *I exist,* to take
one's place among the multitudes.

Walking near the barn at night I feel
the touch of those unable to touch,
of those whose bodies felt too heavy:

finger of cold, finger of dampness.
What have they found courage to ask
now the chance of answering has passed?

LULLABY

The zero of a yawn eclipses your face,
feeling drowsy, eyelids heavy:
goodnight, goodnight, blow out the light,
the century is going to sleep.
Goodnight, Adolf, you almost prevailed—
your dreams, little fellow, rose to fact
like a swamp beast from the muck, then
they settled back again: good luck for us,
bad luck for you, the century is going
to sleep. And Uncle Joe, your musings
tried to duplicate the density of concrete.
Should we add up the dead millions squeezed
like dry leaves to make your diamond?
But then, oh happy day, you passed away.
Dead brutes, dead bullies, the tyrants
totter past to forgottenhood, the century
is going to sleep. But also the heroes:
Babe Ruth, General MacArthur, Gypsy Rose Lee.
The stages you danced upon are compost now,
the newspapers headlining your exploits
pack the landfill. You imitate your shadows.
All the radio broadcasts have been silenced.
Hush! The century is going to sleep.
Ezra Pound, are you still grinding your teeth?
Robert Frost, is your bricklike heart
the only solid chunk left in your coffin?
Thelonious Monk, are you still bopping
someplace down below? Lady Day hums the tune:
lullabies, lullabies, the century
is going to sleep. And all the objects:

the Model T Fords, the 45-rpm records,
eight-track tape players—see them drowsing
in cobwebbed warehouses. Even the rats put a paw
to their lips. The century is going to sleep.
Maybe in another world John Kennedy was never shot,
maybe John Berryman lived a few years longer,
wrote a villanelle before downing Seconal.
And John Lennon, maybe in another world
the madman missed and more songs got made.
All the Johns, all the Janices, all the Sylvias—
blow out the light, the century is going to sleep.
Dead best-sellers, dead Nobel winners,
dead Academy Award winners, dead football
heroes, World Series champions, Kentucky
Derby winners: all tucked between warm sheets,
sweet dreams carouse across their brains.
My father, my grandparents, my cousins,
your faces slide away in the vapor. How
difficult to see you in memory anymore. You
are the frames from which a photo was stolen.
Or my friends, I have left behind too many—
their stories stopped before mine, their
straight lines banked up at black conclusions:
goodnight Ray, goodnight Betty, goodnight Dick,
the century is going to sleep. And those ideas,
the glad ones, the young ones—integration,
human rights. Goodnight, goodnight. The twelve-
tone scale, abstract expressionism. Sweet dreams,
sweet dreams. A chicken in every pot, two cars
in every garage, three TVs in every house.
Sleep tight, sleep tight. We are retreating
to books, electronic texts, some get paragraphs,
some sentences, some footnotes, most get silence.
Shouldn't we walk on tiptoe, shouldn't we whisper?

Do you have sand in your eyes, little fellow?
Let's take a breather. A baby's about to be born.
I won't see much of this one. Maybe a morsel,
if I'm lucky, of its infancy. This next one
belongs to my children and their children. What
Auschwitzes and Hiroshimas are already being
prepared? What will be the carnage of tomorrow?
What dumb ideas will be used to erase human breath?
But also the good stuff: what jokes, what
laughter, what kisses, will there still
be kisses? Better not know, better let it come,
like always, as a surprise. Feeling frightened?
Are you scared? Blow out the light, goodnight,
goodnight, the century is going to sleep.

for Stephen King

WHEN A FRIEND

When a friend dies, part
of oneself splits off
and spins into the outer dark.
No use calling it back.
No use saying I miss you.
Part of one's body has been riven.
One recollects gestures,
mostly trivial. The way
he pinched a cigarette,
the way he crouched on a chair.
Now he is less than a living flea.
Where has he gone, this person
whom I loved? He is vapor now;
he is nothing. I remember
talking to him about the world.
What a rich place it became
within our vocabulary. I did not
love it half so much until
he spoke of it, until it was sifted
through the adjectives of our discussion.
And now my friend is dead.
His warm hand has been reversed.
His movements across a room
have been erased. How I wish
he was someplace specific. He
is nowhere. He is absence.
When he spoke of the things
he loved—books, music, pictures,
the articulation of idea—
his body shook as if a wire

within him suddenly surged.
In passion, he filled the room.
Where has he gone, this friend
whom I loved? The way he shaved,
the way he cut his hair, even
the way he squinted when he talked,
when he embraced idea, held it—
all vanished. He has been reduced
to memory. The books he loved,
I see them on my shelves. The words
he spoke still group around me. But
this is chaff. This is the container
now that heart has been scraped out.
He is defunct now. His body is less
than cinders; less than a sentence
after being whispered. He is the zero
from which a man has vanished. He
was the smartest, most vibrant,
like a match suddenly struck, flaring;
now he is sweepings in a roadway.
Where is he gone? He is nowhere.
My friends, I knew a wonderful man,
these words approximate him,
as chips of stone approximate
a tower, as wind approximates a song.

for Ellis Settle, 1924–1993

HIS DECISION

After his stroke (it was a tiny one),
a minuscule black spot came to rest
within his left eye, seeming to float
upon the cornea. Soon he understood
that death had come to reassure him

of his eventual passage, as if this black
speck were an emblem of what lay beyond.
Like a leaf on a pond, it drifted across
whatever took his attention, the face
of his wife, the delicate and wondering

faces of his children. How small it looked.
Was this the thing of which he had been afraid?
Of course, because of its size, it also seemed
harmless and the idea of its being a doorway
was clearly ridiculous, because who

could squeeze through such a tiny space?
In this way he became accustomed to it.
So later when it grew swollen and enormous,
when it beckoned him between its black portals,
it would seem a doorway he already knew,

like one he had noticed on the street, ornate
and antique, an entrance which had aroused
his curiosity and which today he has decided
to pass through—not summoned, it was something
of his choosing, he felt certain of it.

HUNTING THE MONSTER

You might think the hardest part
is finding its hiding spot. Not true.
What's hard is finding where it's not.

Any street will take you there, any
footpath through the forest. I ask
if you are armed. You lift your weapons.

I turn away and smile. Let's see your
muscles, I say. You strip to the waist.
Clearly you have spent your whole life

preparing. I shrug and we continue.
As guide, I greatly pity these dreamers,
their restless souls, their visions

of better futures. Today we find
the monster in a meadow. I would describe
its dreadful aspect but to each person

it assumes a different shape. To me
it resembles a great mound of gelatin,
to another: a beautiful man or woman,

or a dog with three heads, even a child.
The hunter suggests we proceed on tiptoe.
I say, Why bother? Then the monster

turns toward us and smiles. I find it hard
to convey the sweetness of its expression,
its sheer compassion. The hunter shoots

his gun, fires his arrows, hurls his knife.
Each hits the monster with a plop,
then disappears like a brick into water.

The monster continues to grin. The hunter
flings stones, sticks, clods of dirt.
The hunter attacks with his fists, his boots.

The monster chuckles. At last the hunter
stumbles back. An ambulance is waiting.
The hunter is taken away weeping. I check

my appointment book for the next champion.
Tell me, is this not what it's like to live
in what boasts of being a civilized country?

MIDDLE-AGED BLACK MEN

Here is the sea and here a boat upon the sea
with its jib and mainsail thick with wind. Then
the sails go slack as it comes about. Whitecaps
fleck the water as the boat zigzags across it.

Here a jazz band sets down rhythm and melody
as a middle-aged black man solos on the saxophone.
This is Johnny Hodges and his notes cut across
the music like a sailboat across rough water.

My father has brought me to a concert in the garden
of the Crane estate north of Boston: Duke Ellington
and his big band. This in 1958
and I am seventeen. You recall how Crane toilets

put a little crane on the porcelain? I can never
use one and not think of that night: a huge
château above the ocean, rows of folding chairs
facing the music shell, a concert hall framed

by tall privet. It was August and hot—air
like moist velvet. I wonder about the patience
of my father with a boy who felt like the rhino
in the Kipling tale with grit beneath its skin.

Here is the sea and here a boat upon the sea.
Ellington was the most dapper man I ever saw
with a voice like the air—moist black velvet.
The soloists I came to know later: Clark Terry,

Paul Gonsalves, Ray Nance, Lawrence Brown. At times
the band was like a train with the solo trumpet
moving like a conductor from seat to seat: *Perdido,*
Things Ain't What They Used to Be. At times the sax

was a gull riding air currents above the cliffs.
I sat in front with my feet stretched in the grass.
What I wanted was pattern. All my arguments showed
an endless relativism with one opinion equal

to the next. It seemed I had to find a credible
lie and embrace it. Relativism made it a lie.
But could any lie be a shelter in which to live?
My father refused to argue. Instead, he took me

to hear jazz: Stan Kenton, Cozy Cole at the Metropole
and Mr. Ellington weaving patterns across the dark.
Here was the sea and here a boat upon the sea.
But didn't music distract from what was there,

diverting one's attention from the danger? What
was art but lipstick on a skull? Here we sat in this
gigantic bowl of darkness and in one lit corner
sixteen black men played *Take the A Train,* the theme

with which they began and ended the set, starting
with six full notes, a rough knocking on the door
of night. Most of these men have since joined the night,
my father among them. The seamlessness of nothingness,

didn't the dark make a contrary pattern? What did
it mean to hurl bits of artifice against the night?
Was this foolish or defiant, demented or brave?
At seventeen I was always hanging on tight,

attracted to the abyss and terrified of the abyss.
Wasn't the abyss the rest of my life or no life
at all? Nothing making sense, no muscle in the world.
Here was the sea and here a boat upon the sea.

But perhaps one could enter a poem, piece of music,
even a painting as entering a house, so that one
was surrounded by elaborate architecture and order,
language and light, shape imposed on noise and color.

What made the lie defensible was the joy taken
in the lie, past and future swept away. This idea
didn't come that evening. It was only a beginning.
But there was Duke Ellington and a bunch of old guys,

playing *Rockin' and Rhythm* and *Cop-Out* and nothing
existed beyond them, nothing behind, nothing ahead,
no meanness, nothing cruel. I stared out at the dark
where the ocean lay: the soft palpability of the air,

the smells of pine and salt, a corner of light
on a dark sphere, while the band conjured this vast
body of water and Hodges' sax zigzagged across it—
here was the sea and here a boat upon the sea.

for Hayden Carruth

QUIET TIME

Burdened by hazards the future seems to hold
and dragging his feet by the Scean Gates,
Hector is met by his brother Paris,
just come from his wife, or rather

Menelaus's wife, the root of the trouble:
even in the midst of battle he must fuck her.
Hector has just seen his own wife and son,
and believes he will never see them again.

He thinks that worse than his death, worse
than the destruction of Troy, will be
his wife's captivity—a slave to the Greeks.
"Your Hector, wrapped in everlasting sleep,

shall neither hear you sigh, nor see you weep"—
or so Mr. Pope has made him speak. And standing
by the gates, Hector ponders an idea like that
when Paris runs up to apologize for being late.

Paris thinks that Hector waits because of him,
just as the war is because of him, that he is
the sun around which these planets circulate.
"Impossible man!" says Hector. Two brothers,

one looking outward, the other always in.
And isn't this the way with humankind?
The one who takes the world as his burden,
the other who is the burden of the world—

balance versus imbalance, restraint versus
appetite? We envy Paris his heady rapture,
meaning not just Helen, but the pleasure
of being reckless, the conduct that keeps us

incompletely civilized, yet reconciles us
to our barbarity, the sin acceptable
by seeming huge, Paris's criminal couplings
being his diversion and the tabloid world's.

But Hector spends one last night with his wife
at the end of the next book, a scene which Homer
decides to conceal from us, and Mr. Pope writes,
"All night they feast, the Greek and Trojan powers,

those on the field, and these within their towers."
Hard to picture how Hector holds his infant son,
how he touches his wife's cheek and presses
his body next to hers in the night: as if tumult

were the price paid out for such a quiet time.
No calm without carnage, no carnage without calm:
the twin arcs composing life's single circle.
The next day Hector returns to the killing,

trying to make this world go right again,
which it resists and still resists: a chariot
pulled this way and that, the driver dead,
the horses running loose over the bloody plain.

CRIMSON INVITATION

More sex, more books, more cake, more murder—
consider the invitation to do it all again,
could it be that some might refuse the journey?
What does the cruel soul have to look forward to
but further cruelty? Why should the shy soul
locate itself in one more clumsy body?
The suicides, the downcast, the rejected—
why should they return if they can remain
bodiless, carried aloft as specks of light?
What must have happened not to want it again?
Never to watch the sun sink into the sea,
never to embrace, never to live again.
The beggar, would he refuse the journey?
The woman who lost her children, the man
whose dear love ran off with another? Yesterday
a drop of semen, tomorrow a handful of ash—
so Marcus Aurelius tells us. But consider
all that comes between, the fleeting, the sweet,
never to be repeated, never to happen again.

I think of skiing through the woods in winter,
a few sparrows and chickadees in the branches,
sunlight glistening on the snow, rabbit tracks,
the whisper of trickling water beneath the ice,
the silence rising into the blue bowl of sky.
What does it mean never to want it again?
I think of the faces of my children, the caress
of my wife's fingertips against my cheek. Yesterday
a drop of semen, tomorrow a handful of ash.
Is Marcus Aurelius's dark soul still a point of light

carried aloft by currents of wind? I want them
all to want it again, not just the happy ones
or thoughtless ones or the ones who believed
themselves successful. For even one to hang back
creates a shard of doubt, a stone in the shoe.

But where are the arguments for continuation?
I think of the cemetery in Santiago, the weeping
stone dryads, inconsolable hounds in white marble,
all the bad poetry of loss. I think of the ocean,
how the waves continue the planet's heartbeat,
the line of sandpipers weaving their long dance
at the line of white water. Then to the center
of the city where one can't take a step without
the tall and short, rich and impoverished careening
off one's body, the pushing and bumping, the smell
of sweat and body dirt. Then to the slaughterhouse.
Do you see at this open doorway the steaming table
of livers and lungs, kidneys and guts? A woman
with a white cap and red-smeared apron lifts this
scarlet mass with both hands, offers the ghastly
and lovely, this rich and conflicted invitation
to the planet.
          Beauty fades, cruelty surfaces,
selfishness at last overwhelms. There is only
the journey, a constant on-goingness. Yet often
the image comes of a boat pulling from shore,
the creak of oars, while remaining on the sand
a man and woman stare out at the water, shading
their eyes. The sun is setting, the weather mild.
They watch the boat with its cargo of souls getting
ever smaller as it slides into deepening water.
The couple turns away. Tall palms rise above them.
The man rests his hand upon the woman's shoulder.

The woman puts her arm around the man's waist,
as slowly they enter the shelter of the trees.

Each moment accommodates an eternity. See it
as a small room with two doors. Someday we will
enter to find the second door locked against us.

Now the sun balanced on the horizon seems deformed,
no longer round, as if being pushed down against
the surface of the water. If anyone were left
to witness, he or she might feel wonder, even fear,
as the sun sank into the water as if for forever.

ABOUT THE AUTHOR

Stephen Dobyns teaches in the MFA program at Warren Wilson College. He is the author of eight previous volumes of poetry and seventeen novels. His first book of poems, *Concurring Beasts*, was the Lamont Poetry Selection for 1971. *Black Dog, Red Dog* was the winner of the 1984 National Poetry Series competition. *Cemetery Nights* was chosen for the Poetry Society of America's Melville Cane Award in 1987. His book of essays on poetry, *Best Words, Best Order*, is being published concurrently by St. Martin's Press.